Dear Reader,

I have a weak spot for stories about the feisty heroine butting heads with the wisecracking hero. You just know they're going to wind up in love, but the fun is in the journey. I'm not always sure how they'll arrive at their destination. Some personalities are so strong, they dictate their own stories. Those are the ones I really love because then I'm just the caretaker of the computer, typing madly to keep up with the voices in my head.

Here we have Taylor McIntyre, Brian Cavanaugh's oldest stepdaughter, involved in a mysterious ritual-death case. Her first suspect, J. C. Laredo, turns out to be a private investigator looking into the victim's death as a favor to the grandfather who raised him. Every time Taylor turns around, Laredo keeps popping up and she finds that she can either arrest him for invading the scene of the crime or work with him. As more bodies turn up, she picks the latter. And gets far more than she ever bargained for.

I hope you enjoy this story and, from the bottom of my heart, I wish you someone to love who loves you back.

Marie Ferrarella

USA TODAY BESTSELLING AUTHOR

MARIE FERRARELLA

The Cavanaugh Code

Silhouette®
Romantic
SUSPENSE

SILHOUETTE BOOKS

ISBN-13: 978-0-373-27657-8

Recycling programs
for this product may
not exist in your area.

THE CAVANAUGH CODE

Visit Silhouette Books at www.eHarlequin.com

Printed in U.S.A.

Books by Marie Ferrarella

MARIE FERRARELLA

This *USA TODAY* bestselling and RITA® Award-winning author has written almost two hundred books for Silhouette Books, some under the name Marie Nicole. Her romances are beloved by fans worldwide. Visit her Web site at www.marieferrarella.com.

To Charlie,
who I love more today
than yesterday,
but not half as much as tomorrow.

Chapter 1

The way Detective Taylor McIntyre liked to work a homicide was to put herself in the victim's place. Not just into his or her place, but into their actual lives.

To get a full sense of the person, she needed to walk through their homes, touch their things and imagine what it felt like to be this person who had fallen victim to a homicide.

In essence, Taylor, a third-generation law enforcement agent, wanted to walk in their shoes and examine what they normally had to deal with on a daily basis. She couldn't accomplish that from a distance. And she had come to learn that sometimes the smallest of details was what eventually allowed her and her partner to find the killer and solve the crime.

Just because her partner, Detective Aaron Briscoe,

was on a temporary leave of absence, immersing himself in the head-spinning roller-coaster ride of first-time fatherhood, and the precinct was shorthanded, didn't mean that she had to change her approach. She just had to go through the paces alone rather than have Aaron stare at her as she wandered around, patiently waiting until she needed to use him as her sounding board.

Taylor had no doubt that her partner of almost three years considered her approach unusual, but he'd made his peace with it and generally went along with her method. That was what had made them such a good team and she missed him now, missed the sound of Aaron's grunting as he squatted down to examine something close-up.

She even missed the way Aaron sometimes unconsciously whistled through his teeth, even though it had driven her crazy periodically.

Taylor half smiled to herself as she pulled up in front of an impressive, sprawling four-story apartment complex where the cheapest lease went for the paltry sum of $4,000 a month.

You just never know, do you? she mused. Right now, she'd welcome that awful sound Aaron made. It meant that he was thinking. And two heads were always better than one.

Entering the parking structure, she drove underground and parked in one of the spots designated for guests. Taylor got out and walked toward the elevator located against the back wall.

The late Eileen Stevens's apartment was on the fourth floor. That made it The Villas—as this particular complex was whimsically named—penthouse. And, given the fact that the building was situated at the crest of a hill, anything above the second floor actually had a decent view of the ocean in the distance.

The Villas, a nine-month-old complex with rounded corners and panoramic windows, was situated directly across the street from a newly constructed, exceedingly popular outdoor mall. The mall boasted pricey stores of all sizes, exotic restaurants, a twenty-one-screen movie-theater complex and even had a merry-go-round located smack in the middle. It also promised a skating rink for the winter months. With Christmas less than a month away, there was one now. Hordes of humanity seeking entertainment and diversion swarmed there every Friday and Saturday night. The rest of the week saw a healthy dose of foot traffic, but it was the weekends that put the mall on the map.

Eileen Stevens would no longer be among the people frequenting that mall, Taylor thought, getting out on the fourth floor. Because Eileen Stevens, thirty-eight-year-old dynamo and newly made partner at her prestigious law firm, was found dead in her opulent, cathedral-ceilinged bedroom this morning. With a key to the apartment for emergencies, her personal assistant had come by to see why Eileen hadn't shown up at the firm this morning and wasn't answering her pager or her cell phone.

Upon seeing her dead boss, the young woman, Denise Atwater, had become so hysterical she'd had to be sedated by one of the paramedics summoned to the scene.

Death could be ugly, Taylor thought.

Marble met her heels. The resulting contact created a soft, staccato sound as she made her way from the elevator to Eileen's apartment. In direct contrast to the holly decorating the walls, yellow tape was stretched out across the extra wide door, warning everyone that a crime had been committed here and that they were not allowed to cross the line.

With a sigh, Taylor lifted the tape, slipped beneath it and began to unlock the door. As she turned the key, she realized that there was no need. Someone had failed to lock up.

Sloppy.

Probably a patrolman. Good help was hard to find these days, she mused wryly. But then, life moved at such a fast clip, everyone she knew was juggling three things at once. Oversights were no longer as rare as they had once been. Made the job that much harder to do.

According to the thumbnail bio she'd gotten from the woman's law firm, Eileen Stevens was currently juggling twice that. A criminal lawyer intent on leaving her mark on the world—and making a great deal of money while she was at it—Eileen was regarded as being at the top of her game. The list of clients that the law firm's office manager had surrendered earlier indicated that all of Eileen's clients were high-profile people, people who could pay top dollar for top-notch representation.

Someone obviously didn't think that Eileen was so "top-notch."

Closing the door behind her, Taylor stood for a moment just inside the foyer, trying to imagine what it felt like to come here at the end of a long, bone-wearying day. A sense of antiseptic sterility slowly penetrated her consciousness. Even the Christmas tree, silver with ice-blue decorations, felt sterile as it stood aloof in the center of the room.

"Home" to her had always meant a feeling of warmth and security.

Well, not always, Taylor silently amended.

A feeling of warmth and security was the atmosphere her mother strove to create for her and her three siblings when they were growing up. It had actually been achieved only when her father was out on assignment. An undercover cop, his work would take him away for weeks at a time. Her mother, Lila, also on the police force, came home nightly, no matter what. She was there to check their homework, to make sure they behaved. There to give them the love and support they needed so that they could turn out to be decent human beings.

To give him his due, her father had been an okay guy in the beginning. Taylor could remember laughter in the house when she was very young. But the laughter faded in the later years as jealousy started to eat away at her father. He blamed it on her mother's partner, Brian Cavanaugh, a kind, handsome man who came off larger than life. Initially friends, it got to the point that her father loudly complained that he couldn't compete with or compare to Brian. The growing insecurities that haunted her father, giving rise to arguments, made for an atmosphere of almost stifling tension whenever he was home.

And then everything changed.

Her mother was wounded in the line of duty. Lila

McIntyre would have died if Brian hadn't stopped the flow of her blood with his own hands, holding her until the paramedics arrived, refusing to be separated from her even as she was driven to the hospital.

Her father used the incident as an excuse to shame Lila into retiring from the force, saying a mother of small children had no business putting herself in harm's way. Wanting only peace, Lila went along with it for the sake of her marriage—and her children—until Frank, the youngest, was in high school. Against her husband's wishes, she came back to the police department. Trying to compromise, she took a desk job rather than go back on the street.

Life took a few really strange twists and turns after that. Taylor's father, still working undercover, was suddenly executed, a victim of a drug dealer's hostility. Only it eventually turned out that it had been her father who was the hostile one, staging his own death and stealing the enormous amount of money that was to have been used to stage a sting.

In the end, justice was served. Her father was really dead now and Brian Cavanaugh, a man she had tremendous respect and admiration for, was her stepfather. It was only fitting since over the years he had been more of a father to her and her sister and brothers than her actual father had been.

Brian, now chief of detectives, had been the one to send her out on this case. He'd also offered to restructure a few things within the department so that she could have a temporary partner assigned to her until Aaron and his whistling teeth came back.

But she hated disrupting things and said she'd go solo until Aaron's leave of absence was up. Besides, she didn't relish the idea of breaking in someone new, especially if it was just for a finite amount of time. She could muddle through.

Taylor frowned now as she looked around. She had no doubt that what Eileen had probably spent to furnish just the living room could have kept the children of a third-world nation eating oatmeal for breakfast for the next two years. Maybe three. And yet, for all its tasteful, enormously expensive decor, there was absolutely no warmth to be found in the room.

No warmth anywhere, she concluded as she moved about the area with its snowstorm-white furnishing, making her way to a state-of-the-art kitchen that was too immaculate.

All amenities seemed for show, with no soul evident anywhere. Was the late Eileen Stevens an ice princess, or just haughtily devoid of color and shading?

Taylor found herself feeling sorry for the woman.

"What were you trying to prove, Eileen?" she murmured.

Plastic gloves on, Taylor skimmed her fingertips along the pots hanging from the ceiling like so many slavishly dusted, oversize wind chimes. There had to be a reason for all this decadent hemorrhaging of money, she thought.

"What were you trying to make up for? Were you trying to bury your conscience? Or was there an insecure little girl hidden inside those Prada suits, thumbing her nose at anyone and everyone who had ever made fun of her while she was growing up?"

She made a mental note to find out if the woman had any relatives in the area.

Living well was supposedly the best revenge. And although this was not living well—just living expensively—Taylor knew that many felt their success, their actual self-worth, was reflected in the amount of "toys" they managed to amass.

"Didn't do you any good, did it, Eileen, spending money on all this?" she murmured under her breath. "You still turned out to be mortal." She walked back to the living room. "Who got to you, Eileen? Who did this? An ex-lover? A jealous underling you treated like dirt? Or some client who wanted his money back because you couldn't get him off the way you promised?"

She had yet to carefully go through Eileen's caseload. She made a mental note to do that first thing in the morning, review the woman's past clients as well as her current ones. With any luck, by morning the medical examiner would have gotten around to doing the autopsy. He was a prickly man who marched to his own drummer and refused to listen to anyone else's. But he was good.

"She didn't have any lovers."

Her heart instantly jumping up to her throat, Taylor spun around on her heel. She had her weapon out before she completed the turn. Both hands were wrapped around the grip, its muzzle pointed and meaning business, by the time she found herself facing the source of the voice behind her: a tall, good-looking, dark-haired man in his early thirties.

"Hands in the air!" Taylor ordered, aiming her revolver dead center at his head.

Rather than jump to obey, the stranger watched her as if she was the one who was out of place, not him. "Hey, calm down, honey," he cautioned. "I'm one of the good guys."

Honey?

The hell he was. Taylor found the man's deep, steady voice with its hint of a smile irritating, not to mention patronizing.

Honey? Was he for real?

"Hands in the air!" she ordered again. She cocked the trigger, her blue eyes blazing. "I'm not going to tell you a third time!"

"Yes, ma'am." The stranger acquiesced. But when he raised his hands, they went only as high as his shoulders. At what looked like six-three and in excellent physical condition, he all but towered over her.

There was definitely amusement in his eyes.

Was he a psychopath, coming back to review his handiwork? Eileen Stevens had been found bound and gagged. Cause of death looked like strangulation. From the wet marks on the comforter beneath her body, a wet leather strip had been tightly tied around the woman's throat and then apparently allowed to dry. As it did, it slowly shrank, depriving her of air until she finally choked to death.

It had struck Taylor as a particularly cruel way to kill someone.

Was this man capable of that? She tried her best to make a quick assessment.

In the meantime, more immediate questions needed answering. "What are you doing here?" she demanded.

He began to shrug and drop his hands. She quickly motioned for him to raise them again. Her eyes told him she meant business. Or thought she did. For the sake of peace, he raised his hands again.

"Same as you," he answered casually. "Looking around." And then he added with an amused smile, "Except I'm not talking to myself."

She had no doubt that the man was accustomed to getting along on pure charm. She knew any number of women who would probably go weak in the knees just looking at him.

But the circles she moved around in were full of good-looking men. The Cavanaughs had all but cornered the market and her own brothers didn't exactly look as if their secondary careers involved house haunting. All in all, that made her pretty much immune to the ways of silver-tongued charmers.

Her eyes narrowed now. "No, but you'll talk to me. Turn around," she demanded, whipping out a set of handcuffs from the back of her belt.

The stranger obligingly turned around for her. "Now, nothing kinky," he warned. Taylor found herself wanting to hit him upside his head for his mocking tone. "We haven't even been introduced yet."

As she came close enough to the man to slip on the handcuffs, he suddenly swung around to face her and in a heartbeat, Taylor found herself disarmed. He had the gun now.

"Never let your guard down," he counseled.

The next moment, the tables turned again as the stranger received a sudden, very sharp jab from her knee. Pain shot from his groin into the pit of his stomach, radiating out and making him double over.

"Right," Taylor snapped. "Good advice." She wasted no time as she grabbed one of his wrists, snapping a handcuff into place.

"You're making a mistake," he protested as the second handcuff secured his wrists behind his back.

Taylor rolled her eyes, stepping back and training her gun on him. "Oh, please, I expected something more original than that."

For the first time, the intruder seemed put out, but only marginally, as if he still thought of her as a minor annoyance. "Lady, who kicked you out of bed this morning?"

"That," Taylor informed him crisply, "is none of your business."

The fact that there was no one in her bed, no one currently in her life, was not a piece of information she was about to share with a lowlife, no matter how good-looking he was or how well he dressed. Given the charm he radiated, she pegged him as a successful con artist.

The stranger shook his head and a sigh escaped his lips. "Okay, let's back up here—"

"Too late," Taylor countered. She glanced around to see if anything had been moved from this afternoon, when she'd first come on the scene. It didn't appear so, but she couldn't swear to it. "This is a crime scene and nobody's supposed to be here."

"You are," he pointed out glibly, trying to look at her over his shoulder.

Taylor couldn't resist tossing her head and saying, "I'm special."

He eyed her for a long moment. "No argument, but—"

The smile on his lips went down clear to her bones. Taylor shook the effects off, but it wasn't as easy as she would have liked.

"No *but*," she said sharply. "Just move. Now," she underscored.

He took a step toward the door, then glanced at her again. "Okay, but I have a perfectly good reason for being here."

Taylor fought the temptation to jab him in the ribs with the muzzle of her gun. "This is a roped-off crime scene. There *is* no perfectly good reason to be here— unless you're Santa Claus making an early pit-stop or you're a cop." Her eyes swept over him. "You're definitely not Santa Claus. Are you a cop?" she demanded, knowing perfectly well that he wasn't. She knew all the cops on the force, and, due to her mother's marriage, was now related to more than just a few of them. Even if she hadn't known so many, she would have taken notice of this one had he been on the force.

But he wasn't. She'd never laid eyes on him until a couple of minutes ago.

"No," he answered as nonchalantly as if he were taking a telephone survey, the outcome of which had absolutely no consequence in his life.

"Then, *again,* you shouldn't be here. Now *move.*" She brought her face closer to his. "Don't make me tell you again."

The expression in his eyes said that he knew he could take her. Even with his hands secured behind his back.

But then he merely shrugged and grinned affably—as well as irritatingly.

"No, ma'am," he answered in a voice that was far too polite to be believable, "you won't have to tell me again. I'm moving. See?" he pointed out. "Feet going forward and everything."

What kind of a wise guy was he? Taylor wondered. In the next moment, she silently answered her own question. The kind, she realized, stopping dead, who had managed to get her to stop her normal mode of investigation.

For a reason?

Was there something this man didn't want her to see? *Was* he the killer? Or could he be working for the killer? Had he hidden something, or had she come in time to stop him?

"Hold it," she ordered.

The stranger turned around to look at her. "Come to your senses?" he asked mildly.

"Never left them," Taylor informed him tersely.

Moving behind him, she removed one handcuff and then, rather than undo the other the way she knew he expected, she cuffed his hands around the Doric column that rose up from the center of the living room like an ambiguous statement.

"Now you stay here until I'm finished."

To her surprise, he offered no protest, no angry words at being shackled in this manner. Instead, he merely watched her for another long moment, then asked, "And just what is it you're going to be doing?"

Why did that sound so damn sexy? As if he was implying that she was about to have her way with him instead of just surveying the apartment the way she intended?

It occurred to Taylor that she didn't know his name and hadn't even asked. But then, she had no doubt that he would probably just give her an alias. There was no point in asking.

"What I came here to do," was all she said.

"Then I'm guessing it doesn't have anything to do with me."

"First right answer of the evening," Taylor replied curtly. About to walk away, she stopped and tested the integrity of the handcuffs—just in case. To her satisfaction, they didn't budge. "Now stay put. I'll be back when I'm finished."

"I'll be waiting," he called out after her.

"Damn straight you'll be waiting," Taylor muttered under her breath in exasperation as she walked out of the room and headed for Eileen Stevens's bedroom.

The last place the criminal lawyer had gone alive.

Chapter 2

Taylor stood in the walk-in closet that was bigger than her own bedroom. Surveying its contents, she shook her head.

How did one woman manage to accumulate so many clothes? Moreover, nearly half of them still had their tags on. Eileen hadn't even gotten around to wearing them yet.

Was there some inner compulsion that made her just buy things to have them, not necessarily to use them?

"Who's going to wear them now, Eileen?" Taylor asked softly, examining a designer original evening gown that sparkled even in the artificial overhead light. "What drove you, Eileen? What?"

Taylor stopped talking and cocked her head, listening. Was that...?

It was.

The sound of the front door opening and then closing. Instantly alert, her journey in the other woman's shoes immediately suspended, Taylor pulled out her weapon again.

Had someone else come in?

What was going on here, anyway? It felt as if she'd wandered into an open house instead of an official crime scene. Holding her breath, Taylor cautiously made her way to the living room again.

And then stopped dead.

The handcuffs she'd used to secure the intruder were neatly lying on the white rug before the Doric column, nothing but air held within the metal circles.

She rushed over to the cuffs and grabbed them, exasperation bubbling within her veins as she scanned the room. The intruder was nowhere to be seen. He'd pulled a Houdini on her. How? These weren't fake cuffs or a prop. The average person couldn't have gotten out of them.

Hell, *she* couldn't have gotten out of them. But he had. Just who the hell *was* he?

"Damn it!" Taylor exclaimed, scanning the room again as if the second survey would somehow uncover the man for her.

What if the door opening and closing was just to throw her off?

She looked around for a third time, tension weaving in and out of her. Taylor half expected the stranger to come charging at her from one of the corners.

Adrenaline still rushing through her veins, weapon drawn, she swept from one room to another, checking closets, bathrooms, the balcony. Anywhere the man could have folded his lengthy form and attempted to hide. All to no avail.

The man was gone.

Who the hell was he and how did he fit into all this? she silently demanded, her exasperation growing exponentially. This scenario wouldn't have gone this way if Aaron had been with her. Damn him, anyway.

No, Taylor upbraided herself tersely the next moment. This wasn't Aaron's fault, it was hers. She was the one who'd gotten sloppy, unconsciously getting too accustomed to someone having her back at all times.

She knew better.

On this job, no matter what, you had to remain vigilant because there were no guarantees and even the best of partners could be caught napping.

Just like she had this evening, she thought in disgust.

Crossing to the front door, Taylor locked it, then tested the doorknob to make sure it held. It did. Even so, she dragged one of the chairs over and placed it in front of the ornate door. If "Houdini" decided to come back and pick the lock, he'd still wind up hitting the chair. The scraping noise the feet would make against the marble would alert her. She didn't want to be caught off guard a second time.

Most likely, she mused, the intruder wasn't going to come back. He was probably just happy to get away. Not that she planned to let him. She intended to find him, but that was something she'd deal with later. *After* she did what she came here to do.

Glancing toward the door one final time, Taylor went

back to Eileen Stevens's bedroom. Somewhere amid all the woman's things she hoped to get a handle on the late lawyer's life.

No doubt about it, Eileen Stevens had led an extremely busy life, Taylor concluded more than ninety minutes later, finally driving home to her own apartment. A busy life, but, as far as she could ascertain, it had been far from satisfying. The few photographs that did grace the walls in the lawyer's study were of Eileen and the other, older partners from the firm. Eileen appeared very formal in them.

Didn't the woman have a personal life?

From everything she'd found, it didn't seem so. There were no love letters stashed in a bottom drawer, held fast with a faded ribbon, no secret photographs tucked away in an album of someone who had once made her pulse race. There was nothing to indicate that Eileen had made any kind of personal contact with anyone.

The only scrapbook the woman had kept was filled with newspaper articles about her cases. Cases she had won. It was all about winning for Eileen.

Can't take a court victory to bed with you at night, Taylor thought.

"Looks like you lost, big time," Taylor murmured under her breath to a woman who could no longer benefit from any insight she might have to give.

Is this any better than your life? an annoying voice in her head mockingly asked. *Here it is, way past your shift, and what are you doing? Poking around a dead woman's apartment.*

Taylor unconsciously stiffened her shoulders. Eileen Stevens's life *wasn't* like her life, she silently insisted. *She* had a life, *she* had a family. A family that meant the world to her and who were always there for her anytime she needed them, or just wanted to kick back. Just because she wasn't spending her nights with a lover didn't make her anything like the dead woman.

She blew out a breath as she pulled into her apartment complex, a modest collection of garden apartments with carport parking and bright white daisies planted all along their borders.

"Great, so now you're arguing with yourself. Maybe you *should* go back to Brian and have him assign that temporary partner to you," she said out loud in disgust.

Taylor pulled into her carport and turned the engine off. For a second she sat there, listening to crickets calling to each other. In the distance was not-so-faint music coming from the pool area. Someone was having another party.

Someone was *always* having another party this time of year. She felt no desire to go.

Maybe you should go, anyway. Might do you good.

She shook her head. Andrew Cavanaugh saw to her social life. The former chief of police and family patriarch held enough gatherings at his place to take care of any spare time she had.

Tonight she was just tired. Tired and disappointed in herself for allowing that cocky intruder to get away. *Tomorrow would be better,* she silently vowed getting out of her vehicle. All she needed was a good night's sleep and then she'd be back on track.

The good night's sleep she'd planned on had eluded her.

Oh, she'd slept all right, but rather than a restful, dreamless event, her night was packed full of dreams. One dream flowering instantly into another, all involving the sexy intruder.

The dreams played out so vividly that she'd had trouble separating reality from fiction. In several versions, the intruder got the drop on her rather than she on him. In the last dream, things inexplicably heated up. Her clothes disappeared just as she realized that he wasn't wearing any either.

That was when she bolted upright, waking up.

It was 7:00 a.m. and her pulse was racing. Her breathing was so shallow she thought for a moment she was going to hyperventilate. The downside was that she felt far more tired than when she'd first fallen asleep.

Exhausted, her breathing finally under control, she dropped, face forward on the comforter for a moment longer.

Who the hell was that man and how did he fit into Eileen's life? Taylor wondered for the hundredth time.

She knew she wasn't going to have any peace until she answered those questions, especially the first one. Sitting up again, Taylor sighed and dragged her hand through her tousled, long blond hair. First thing this morning, she would see about getting together with the sketch artist, before the intruder's features faded from her memory.

She should be so lucky.

Throwing off the covers, Taylor marched into the bathroom. She rushed through her shower and was drying off in less than ten minutes. Dressed, she ran her fingers through her hair as she aimed the hair dryer at several sections, impatient to be on her way. She was determined to find out the man's name and bring him in before the day was out.

Breakfast was a banana she peeled and ate between leaving her front door and reaching her vehicle in the carport.

She was on her way to the precinct less than half an hour after she'd woken up.

Tracking down the mysterious intruder turned out to be a lot easier than she ever imagined.

Arriving at the precinct, Taylor went straight up to her squad room. Her intention was to drop off her purse at her desk and then go in search of the sketch artist.

She stopped dead ten feet short of her goal.

The intruder was there, sitting in the chair beside her desk, looking as if he didn't have a care in the world.

Taylor's first instinct was to draw her weapon, but she banked it down even though training a gun on him would have been immensely satisfying. The man obviously wasn't a criminal. A criminal didn't just waltz into a squad room and make himself at home. Although, approaching the scene from another angle as she played her own devil's advocate, that could actually be the perfect cover.

Either way, the stranger obviously had a hell of a lot of nerve.

Taking a deep breath, Taylor crossed the rest of the way through the room to her desk.

As if sensing her presence, the stranger turned his head and looked right into her eyes a moment before she reached him.

"You," she spat out, making the single word sound like an angry accusation.

An accusation that apparently left him unruffled. The stranger merely smiled that maddening smile she'd previewed last night.

"Me," he affirmed.

Instead of throwing her purse into the bottom drawer, she dropped it in. But she satisfied her need to blow off steam by kicking the drawer shut.

"Who the hell are you?" she demanded, barely keeping her voice down. "And how did you get out of those handcuffs?"

"Handcuffing your dates these days?"

Focused only on the stranger, Taylor almost jumped. The question came from her brother, Frank, another homicide detective. Frank had chosen that moment to come up behind her. Fresh off solving a serial-killer case and riding the crest of triumphant satisfaction, her younger brother grinned at her.

"You know the department frowns on taking their equipment for personal use." He moved so that he stood next to the annoying stranger.

Taylor struggled to keep from telling her brother to butt out. "This isn't a date, this is a suspect," she bit off.

"A suspect?" the intruder echoed, still smiling that annoyingly sexy smile that seemed to undulate right under her skin, shooting straight to her core and warming it. "For what?" he asked innocently.

As if he didn't know. "For the murder of Eileen Stevens," she snapped.

"A suspect?" her brother repeated in disbelief, then looked, stunned, at the seated man. "Laredo?"

Taylor's eyebrows narrowed over eyes the color of the midmorning sky. "Who the hell is Laredo?" she demanded.

"I am," the stranger told her affably. The next moment, he half rose in his seat and extended his hand to her. "J. C. Laredo," he introduced himself. "I came in to see if we might be able to have a successful exchange of information. I would have asked last night," he went on, "but you looked a little too hot and perturbed to listen to reason."

"Taylor hardly ever listens to reason," Frank told the man as if he was sharing some sort of a family confidence.

"Taylor also has excellent hearing and is standing right here," she pointed out angrily to her brother, struggling to hang on to her temper.

She felt Laredo's eyes slide over her torso as they took full measure of her. Slowly they went from her head down to her toes. It took all she had not to shiver.

"You most certainly are," Laredo agreed in a voice that told her he highly approved of the body he'd just inventoried.

Frank leaned his head in toward Laredo and said, "I think you got her angry. I'd be careful if I were you. Taylor bites heads off when she's angry." With that, Frank began to retreat.

"I'll keep that in mind," Laredo promised. His eyes shifted over to Taylor. "Taylor, is it?" he asked, rolling the name over on his tongue as if he were tasting it for sweetness. Satisfied, he smiled. "I think we got off on the wrong foot last night."

Frank was obviously still within hearing range because she heard her brother chuckle to himself and murmur, "Like *that* never happened before."

Taylor took a deep breath, struggling to get her surprisingly frayed temper under control. She was going to kill Frank when she got the chance. Never mind that he was two months shy of his wedding. She'd be doing her almost-sister-in-law a favor. Frank could be godawful annoying when he wanted to be.

"All right," she said, her voice straining to sound civil as she faced the man sitting at her desk. "This is the season for goodwill toward men. I'm listening, Laredo. What were you doing at Eileen Stevens's apartment last night?"

Since the man had gotten out of the handcuffs, she saw no point in asking how he had managed to elude the security guards in the building's lobby. That had obviously been child's play for him.

Laredo answered without missing a beat. "Probably the same thing as you."

She didn't like playing games unless they involved a board and little colored game pieces. "You said you weren't a cop."

The look on his face was innocence personified. "I'm not."

"Then you weren't doing the same thing that I was,"

Taylor concluded curtly. "And you weren't supposed to be there."

Instead of arguing the point with her, Laredo surprised her by nodding his head. But just as she began to wonder why he was being so agreeable, he admitted, "I bent the rules a little. But I am investigating her death."

She highly doubted that there were two investigations going on at the same time. They hardly had enough people to sufficiently cover all the city's crimes now. If another branch of law enforcement was involved, someone would have told the Chief of D's, who in turn would have warned her.

Handsome or not, this character, she concluded, was full of hot air. "By whose authority?" she asked, thinking that she was just giving him enough rope to hang himself.

She wasn't expecting the answer he gave her.

"Indirectly, her mother, Carole Stevens. I'm actually doing this as a favor to my grandfather. He used to date the dead woman's mother," he confided.

Taylor felt far from enlightened. Was this man just making this up and hoping his charm would fill in the gaps?

"You're contaminating a crime scene as a favor to your grandfather?" she challenged incredulously.

"I know enough not to contaminate the crime scene," Laredo assured her in a voice that she found as irritatingly patronizing now as she had the night before. The next moment, he reached into his pocket. Every nerve ending went on the alert and she started to reach for her sidearm out of habit.

Laredo noted her reaction. "Relax," he told her in a voice that could have easily been used to gentle a wild animal. "I'm just reaching for my wallet, not my Saturday night special."

She deeply resented the smirk she heard in the man's voice.

"Do you own one?" she wanted to know.

The term referred to a weapon that was the common choice of thugs and penny-ante thieves more than two decades ago, before far more colorful, sophisticated and seductively affordable weapons hit the streets.

"I own a lot of guns," he informed her easily, placing his wallet, opened and face up, in the middle of her desk.

Taylor looked down at the private investigator's license he was showing her. The photograph in the corner was a surprisingly good one. But then, the thought whispered along the perimeter of her mind, the photograph was of a surprisingly good-looking man.

"John Chester Laredo, private investigator," she read out loud.

Taylor raised her eyes quizzically to his. Chester? Who named their kid Chester these days, even as a middle name?

"That's me," he responded, taking his wallet back and tucking it into his pocket.

Taylor blew out a breath, trying to put a positive spin on things. At least she didn't have to waste time with the sketch artist. Now, instead of arresting the annoying man, she just had to get rid of him.

"All right," she allowed, "for the time being, let's just say you're on the level."

Was it her imagination, or did his grin just get more annoying? "Let's," he agreed.

She frowned. "That still doesn't give you the right to be there, 'bending rules,'" she said sarcastically, "and poking around."

"I wasn't 'poking,'" he corrected affably, "I was looking. And obviously, if I thought the police would object to what I was doing—" he leaned forward slightly "—I wouldn't have come out and made myself known to you last night, now, would I?"

For a second, he had her. She was willing to admit he had a point.

But then, the next moment she realized that there was no way for him to have known that she was with the police department. She could have been with the housing management—or even a thief, drawn to the apartment by the yellow crime scene tape to see what she could make off with.

"You're a little large to hide, even in a place as big as that," she pointed out. "It seems to me, given a choice, you decided that it was best to take the bull by the horns."

His grin was *really* starting to get to her, which made her increasingly uneasy.

"I wouldn't exactly use the term *bull*," Laredo told her. "I have a lot of friends on the force. I didn't think anyone would mind."

Taylor's eyes narrowed. *Think again, Laredo.* She didn't like anyone even remotely messing with her crime scene. "Well, then you thought wrong," she informed him tersely.

Chapter 3

Laredo had gotten to his position in life by reading people correctly. Innate instincts had trained him to be an excellent judge of character. Consequently, he knew when to push and when to step back.

He also knew when a little extra persuasion might help him wear down barriers. He had a feeling that the sexy-looking blonde with the serious mouth did not respond favorably to being either opposed or coerced.

Moving slightly forward in the chair so that his face was closer to hers, Laredo looked into the woman's eyes. They were a shade lighter than his own. And very compelling. You could tell a lot about a person by the way they looked at you and her eyes never wavered, never looked away.

"C'mon, Taylor," he coaxed, "what's the harm in sharing information?"

She didn't want him getting familiar with her. He wasn't her friend, he was an annoying man and she was still debating having him arrested for tampering with evidence.

"It's Detective McIntyre," she informed him stiffly, and then added, "and I don't talk about ongoing investigations with civilians." And that, she hoped, would bring an end to any further discussion of Eileen Stevens's murder.

The corners of Laredo's mouth curved in what she could only think of as a devilish grin. A wicked expression flared in his eyes as he said, "I'll show you mine if you show me yours."

Taylor would have felt better if she'd thought that the air-conditioning system had broken down that morning. At least then she would have had something to blame for the sudden overwhelming wave of heat surging through her body, leaving no part untouched.

Stalling for time as she tried to get a grip, Taylor blew out a breath. Laredo's eyes, she noted, never left hers.

The way she saw it, she had three ways to go here. She could keep sparring with this annoying private investigator and, most likely, get nowhere while taking precious time away from her investigation. That option held no appeal because she was already behind without a partner's help.

Her second choice was to get someone to eject this overconfident ape from the premises, but she had the uneasy feeling that Laredo wasn't lying about having friends in the department. If he knew her brother, he had to know others as well. Trying to get him thrown out might make her seem like a shrew—and it probably wouldn't work anyway.

Or, door number three, she could toss Laredo a crumb in exchange for finding out exactly what he knew. There was the chance that he had stumbled across something. After all, he had managed to get to Eileen Stevens's penthouse apartment before she had. Who knew how long he'd been there or what he might have seen—and taken?

Door number three it was.

Taylor braced herself. "All right, what do you have?"

She watched as his smile unfurled further. Why did she get the feeling that he was the spider and she was the fly, about to cross the threshold into his open house?

"I believe I said, 'I'll show you mine *if* you show me yours.' That means that you go first, as it should be," he added, "since my mother taught me that it should always be ladies first."

Try as she might, Taylor just couldn't form a mental picture of the woman who'd given birth to this larger-than-life, annoyingly sexy specimen of manhood.

"You have a mother?"

The question had slid from her mind to her tongue before she could stop it. What the hell was he doing to her manners and, more importantly, why was she letting him do it? Once this case was over, she was definitely going on vacation. Her batteries needed recharging.

"Had," Laredo quietly corrected, his seductive grin toning down several wattage levels—and becoming all the more lethal for it.

Taylor did her best to steel herself. For all she knew, Laredo could just be orchestrating this to make her feel guilty. If she felt guilty enough about stumbling onto this sensitive area, he might think she'd fold easily.

It made sense, but even so, she couldn't shake the feeling that she'd just stomped across ground she shouldn't have. She was extremely sensitive when it came to matters that concerned family. Family was, if anything, her Achilles' heel.

Her family was chiefly responsible for who and what she was today. She'd joined the force and become a police detective because her mother had been one before her. And, because of what she'd seen transpiring in her family as a child, she was gun-shy when it came to relationships. The moment one appeared to go beyond being an inch in depth, she bailed, remembering what her mother had gone through with her father. No matter that her mother's second marriage seemed made in heaven; it was the tempestuous first one that had left its indelible mark.

Taylor found it ironic that while she had implicit trust in the men she'd been partnered with when it came to life-and-death situations, she absolutely refused to trust any man with her heart. Taylor staunchly opposed revealing her vulnerability.

Rallying, Taylor squared her shoulders. "Okay, here's what I've got." She deliberately ignored the touch of triumph she saw enter his eyes. "Graduating fifth in her class from Stanford Law School, Eileen Stevens worked her way up extremely fast. She became a much sought-after criminal lawyer who rarely lost a case. None in the last five years. Her list of clients reads like a who's who of the rich and famous—or infamous," she added, thinking of a couple of so-called "wiseguys" who were on the list. "She was made partner at her law firm six months ago. According to the electronic calendar they found by her bed, the woman ate and slept work 24/7. She didn't appear to have a social life that wasn't connected to the firm."

Taylor paused for a moment, wishing she understood how a woman with no social life could end up the victim of a very personal crime. "But someone hated her enough to tie her up and wrap a wet piece of leather tightly around her neck, then wait for the strip to dry and strangle her. My guess is that the process took at least a couple of hours."

"How do you know they waited?"

Laredo didn't look impressed by her conclusion, just mildly curious, like someone asking study questions they already knew the answer to.

She told him anyway. "The carpet is thick and lush— my guess is that it's fairly new. There was a set of shoe prints set in it next to the bed, like someone had stood there for more than just a minute. The killer, watching her die." The comforter beneath the woman's body had been all tangled, as if Eileen had thrashed around while tied to the bedpost, trying to get free, but Taylor didn't add that, waiting to see if Laredo would.

He didn't. Instead, he merely nodded at her narrative. "So far," the private investigator told her, "we're of a like mind."

"And you have nothing to add?" she demanded. He was playing games with her, just trying to find out what she knew. She didn't like being duped.

"I didn't say that," he told her evenly, his gaze locked on hers.

"So?" she asked impatiently.

"I don't have anything from the present—yet," Laredo qualified. "But what I do have is more of a background on Eileen."

Taylor crossed her arms before her, waiting. "Go ahead." It was an order, not a request.

Laredo obliged and recited what he'd learned since his grandfather had come to him with this.

"Eileen Stevens was thirty-eight and the complete epitome of an obsessed career woman. But she wasn't always so goal oriented. When she was a seventeen-year-old high school junior, Eileen got pregnant." He saw the surprise in Taylor's eyes and knew she wouldn't be challenging the worth of the exchange between them. "Her mother wouldn't allow her to have an abortion. The baby, a boy, was turned over to social services the day he was born. From what I gathered, the experience made Eileen do a complete one-eighty. She turned her back on her former wild life and buckled down to become the woman she is today."

"Dead," Taylor couldn't help pointing out.

A hint of a smile touched his lips. "I don't think that was in her plans."

If Laredo was trying to undermine her by laughing at her, he was in for a surprise, Taylor thought. She'd survived growing up with Zach and Frank, expert tormentors both.

"Anything else?"

Laredo spread his hands wide. "That's it so far."

She doubted it, but she had no way of keeping him for interrogation at the moment. "And who did you say you were working for?"

"I'm doing this as a favor," he told her even though he was fairly certain that she hadn't forgotten. She was probably just trying to trip him up, which was all right, he thought, because in her place he probably would have done the same thing. "My grandfather used to date Eileen Stevens's mother. Carole Stevens was a single mother who worked double shifts as a cocktail hostess to make ends meet. That didn't exactly leave her much time to be a parent and from what I gathered, as a kid Eileen needed a firm hand. After she graduated high school, they became estranged for a number of years—"

"Because her mother refused to allow her to have the abortion." Taylor guessed.

Laredo inclined his head. "That was part of it, yes," he acknowledged.

So he did know more than he'd just admitted. "And the rest of it?"

He shrugged. "Just the usual mother-daughter animosity."

She didn't like the way he just tossed that off. Taylor felt her back going up. Something about him made her want to contradict him no matter what he said.

"It's not always 'usual,' Laredo."

Her defensive manner aroused his interest. "You never clashed with your mother for no other reason than just because she was your mother?"

She definitely didn't like his way of stereotyping

people, she thought. "Not that it's any business of yours," she told him coolly, "but no."

He didn't say anything for a moment. It seemed rather obvious to Laredo that Taylor McIntyre was head-strong and stubborn. He couldn't visualize her being easygoing about things and letting them slide unless she wanted to.

"Not once?" he prodded.

"No," she repeated. Less-than-fond memories had her adding, "That was for my father to do." Then, real-izing that she had said far more than she'd wanted to, she shot another question at him. "If Eileen and her mother were so estranged, why is her mother asking you to investigate who killed her daughter? Is there a will involved?"

As far as she knew, the police hadn't even found out that the murder victim had a mother in the state. She'd left her next-of-kin information blank on the law firm's employment form.

"I don't know about a will," Laredo admitted. "But as far as Carole and Eileen's estrangement went, my grandfather said they'd reconciled just a few months ago. According to him, the reconciliation was all Carole's doing," he added. "Carole said she felt that life was too short to let hurt feelings keep people apart. Per-sonally, I think my grandfather gave Carole a little push in the right direction."

For a reason? Taylor wondered. "And your grandfa-ther, how does he figure into all this? Beyond the little push, of course."

Sarcasm always rolled off his back. Most likely, the

long-legged detective was trying to get something more
out of him, some "dirt" she probably thought he'd con-
veniently omitted.

Sorry to disappoint, Taylor, Laredo thought, doing
little to hide his amusement.

"He's just a nice guy who's there for his friends,
that's all."

"Or, in this case," she reminded him, "volunteering
you."

He certainly couldn't argue with that, Laredo
thought. But then, in the scheme of things, it was the
least he could do. If he spent the rest of his life as his
grandfather's right-hand man, he wouldn't begin to
repay the man for everything that he had done for
him.

"Something like that," he agreed.

Time to stop dancing, she decided. She'd already
spent too much time getting next to nothing. "What is
your grandfather's name and where can I find him if I
want to talk to him?"

"His name's Chester Laredo," a familiar, deep voice
behind her said.

Taylor didn't need to turn around to know that the
voice belonged to her stepfather. At the same time, she
thought to herself, so much for the mystery of why
Laredo's middle name was Chester.

The next moment, Brian Cavanaugh, Aurora's chief
of detectives, came around her desk, extending his hand
to the man she'd been trying to pump for information.
Brian smiled broadly at Laredo.

"Frank mentioned he saw you here. How are you,

Laredo?" he asked warmly, shaking the younger man's hand. "And what's your grandfather up to these days?"

"I'm fine and he's been running a security firm for the last five years," Laredo told him, sitting down again.

"A security firm?" Brian laughed, shaking his head. "I never thought he'd leave The Company. I thought they'd have to take him out, feet first."

"He thought it was time," Laredo told him. "He didn't think he could move as fast as he used to."

"Chet?" Brian asked incredulously. "That man could pop open any lock and disappear faster than anyone I ever knew."

That would explain the handcuffs, Taylor suddenly thought. And then the initial sentence played itself over in her head.

"The Company?" Taylor echoed, looking from her stepfather to the man at her desk. "Your grandfather was with the—"

"Yes," Laredo said, cutting her off before she could mention the CIA. "He doesn't like it getting around these days. Afraid it might scare off more clients than it attracts," he explained.

Brian looked as if that made perfect sense to him. "Well, tell him I said hello and if he ever feels like catching up, he knows where to find me."

Okay, this was another new turn, Taylor thought. What did Brian have to do with a member of the CIA? "Catching up?" she asked.

Brian left it deliberately vague. "We collaborated a couple of times back in the day."

Taylor blew out a breath. She wasn't going to get any

more than that and she knew it. For all his affability, Brian Cavanaugh was extremely closemouthed when he wanted to be.

She moved on. "So you're vouching for him?" She nodded at Laredo as she asked.

"Absolutely. I've known Laredo for as long as I've known you," he told her. "Bounced you both on my knee—just not at the same time," Brian added with the wink that she knew was her mother's undoing. Brian shifted his eyes toward Laredo. "If I can help you in any way, just let me know."

"I'll do that," Laredo promised. "But right now, I've got no complaints with the way Detective McIntyre is taking care of me."

Brian smiled, affection brimming in his eyes as he looked at his older stepdaughter.

"Never doubted it for a moment. She's one of our finest. Good seeing you again, Laredo," Brian repeated just as his cell phone began to ring. He sighed. "No rest for the weary," were his parting words as he walked away quickly, taking out his phone. "Cavanaugh here."

"He's a great guy," Laredo said to her. There was genuine admiration in his voice. There, at least, Taylor thought, they were in agreement.

"Yes, I know." She turned her attention back to the man at her desk. "I guess if he vouches for you, I can trust you." She couldn't help the grudging note that came into her voice.

"With your life." Laredo sounded completely serious as he said it.

But she still couldn't help wondering if he meant it, or was trying to throw her off. Ordinarily, if Brian vouched for someone, that was enough for her. But something about the way Laredo looked at her had her struggling to keep her guard up.

For the second time, she told herself to wrap it up. She had witnesses she needed to question and an investigation to kick off. Damn, but she missed Aaron. The man wasn't due back for another six weeks. They stretched out before her like a long, lonely desert.

"All right," she announced to Laredo, "if you have nothing else to tell me—"

The same sexy, lazy smile traveled along his lips, straight into her nervous system.

"I have lots of things to tell you," he assured her, his voice deliberately lower than it had been, carrying only the length of her desk. "Preferably over a lobster dinner with soft music in the background and some champagne chilling beside the table."

Nine times out of ten, that line probably worked, she thought. But not on her. "You're a player."

He smiled. If it bothered him to be caught, he didn't show it. "When the occasion arises. The rest of the time, I'm pragmatic."

You had to admire a guy who didn't give up, she thought despite herself. "And plying me with liquor would be which?"

He looked at her for a long moment before saying, "A little bit of both, most likely."

If she hung around him any longer, she was in danger of getting lost in those blue eyes, Taylor warned herself.

"Well, I have a job to do, so if you'll excuse me." With that, she rose to her feet.

Laredo did the same. And as she went out of the squad room, he was right there, his steps shadowing hers until they both reached the elevator.

She had no recollection of issuing an invitation, Taylor thought.

Pressing the down button, she turned to face him. "Look, if you think you're coming with me just because my stepfather bounced you on his knee—"

A touch of surprise entered his eyes. "Brian Cavanaugh's your stepfather?"

It was something she assumed everyone knew because, in the world she inhabited, for the most part they did. "Yes."

He nodded, as if approving. "Your mother's got a good man."

She was *not* going to get sidetracked. "Be that as it may, you're not coming with me."

"I didn't think I was."

She pressed the down button again. "Then why are you following me?"

"I'm not," he told her innocently.

Where was the damn elevator? There weren't that many floors. "Right."

"In case it might have slipped your notice, 'Detective,' cars are supposed to be parked outside the building and I haven't trained mine to come when I call so, consequently, if I want to use it, I have to go to the car." He gave her an amused look. "Same as you, I suspect."

She was about to press for the elevator a third time

when it arrived. She saw that the car was almost filled to capacity. Ordinarily, she would have waited for the next car, but she wanted to get away from this man as quickly as possible. So she slipped into the car, trying to make the most of the space that was available.

As did he.

Taylor discovered that ignoring a man she found herself pressed up against was next to impossible no matter how hard she tried.

Chapter 4

Hours later, out in the field, Taylor could swear she could still feel the blush from that morning creeping up her neck. It lingered, breathing color along her cheeks as they traveled down in the elevator to the first floor.

To his credit, Laredo had made no reference to being packed against her like an amorous sardine, but it was obvious that he was thinking about it. One look at the smile in his eyes told her that.

Damn annoying man, Taylor thought now, not for the first time. If her stepfather and Frank hadn't indirectly vouched for Laredo by the way they'd both greeted and interacted with the man, J. C. Laredo would have definitely been at the top of her list of suspects to investigate. She wasn't sure if she would have bought into his

story about investigating Eileen's murder as a favor to
his grandfather if it hadn't been for them.

Even so, she still might look into his background
once she finished interviewing the people on the
victim's list of clients. She'd been doing that for a good
part of the day, as well as talking to the other tenants in
Eileen's building. So far, she felt as if she was just
spinning her wheels. Slowly.

After getting back into her car, Taylor closed the
door and then just sat there for a moment, looking over
the remaining names on the list of clients. Because they
were all celebrities of varying degrees, getting past their
bodyguards and arranging for a few minutes of conversation was turning out to be almost a Herculean effort.
She wouldn't mind if she felt that this helped the investigation, but it didn't.

A gut feeling told her that she was probably just wasting
her time. Maybe she needed to talk to Eileen's mother.

That was when it occurred to Taylor that she'd been
so eager to get away from Laredo, she had completely
forgotten to ask for Carole Stevens's address.

With a sigh, she dug out the card the private investigator had pressed into her hand just before they
parted company.

"In case you change your mind and decide you want
to collaborate," he'd said, punctuating his statement
with a rather unsettling wink just before he'd sauntered
off to his car.

She recalled thinking, almost against her will, that
Laredo had the tightest butt she'd ever seen on a man. That
was when she'd almost thrown his card away. But there

weren't any trash containers in the immediate vicinity, so she'd temporarily stuffed it into her jacket pocket.

Looking now at the plain white card with its bold, raised black lettering, Taylor read the cell number twice, repeating it under her breath before putting it into her own phone.

The phone on the other end rang four times. She was fairly certain it would go to voice mail, but then she heard a noise. The next moment, a deep male voice rumbled against her ear and she was certain she had the real deal, not a recording.

"Laredo."

Something suddenly and unexpectedly tightened in her gut. Annoyed with herself—and him—Taylor almost flipped the phone closed. Damn it, she was acting like some indecisive schoolgirl, she upbraided herself. This just had to stop. *Now.*

"That you, Detective McIntyre?" she heard the deep voice ask when the silence stretched out. She could *swear* she heard a smile in his voice.

"Yes," she bit off grudgingly. "It's me." How had he known? It wasn't as if she'd indicated that she was *ever* going to call him, at least, not until such time as the Winter Olympics took place on the frozen terrains of hell.

As if reading her mind, he said, "Didn't expect to hear from you so soon. Miss me?"

"Like a toothache." Taylor could almost see the smirk on his lips. "I need Carole Stevens's phone number and address."

He was the soul of cooperation. "Sure thing. Got a pencil and paper?"

"Of course I do," she answered, quickly opening her glove compartment and tossing things onto the passenger seat in a frenzied attempt to locate the items.

"I can wait," he offered, as if he could see her rummaging.

The man made her exceedingly uneasy. "The address," she repeated, issuing the words like a direct order.

"Yes, ma'am."

Carole Stevens lived in the older part of town, Taylor thought as she wrote down the street address. Had those been Eileen's roots as well? she wondered, quickly writing down the phone number Laredo recited.

"Thanks."

"Anytime, Detective McIntyre," he replied cheerfully.

Last time, Taylor countered mentally. She quickly terminated the connection before he could say anything else.

Why the hell was her heart racing? Taylor silently demanded as she turned the key in the ignition. There was absolutely no reason for it to be beating as if she'd just completed a hundred-meter dash.

She really needed to go on that vacation. The minute that Aaron came back, she would take off for a couple of weeks. Let *him* go solo for a while. It would serve him right, leaving her in a lurch like this.

What *was* the matter with her? Taylor thought the next moment, guiding the car to the main thoroughfare. She was happy for Aaron. She knew how much he and his wife, Rachel, had wanted this baby, how long they had tried to get pregnant. They *deserved* to enjoy their little girl.

Taylor sighed, her hands tightening on the steering wheel. Just when had she turned into the Wicked Witch of the West?

Since her path had crossed Laredo's. There was no point in denying it. She didn't know what it was about the tall, muscular private investigator with the intrusive manner, but he made her feel as if she was walking on a foundation made of gelatin.

What she needed, until she could go off on that mythical vacation, was to hang out a few mornings at Andrew's house. The former chief of police threw his doors open every morning, making gastronomically thrilling breakfasts for whichever member of his family happened to wander into his house. The man loved to cook and he loved his family. And everybody knew that. The atmosphere within Andrew Cavanaugh's house was energizingly positive and right now, she could use a little positive reinforcement.

Since her mother was married to Brian, Andrew's younger brother, that connected her to the family patriarch. Not that she actually needed an excuse to show up. Andrew considered most of the people on the police force his extended family.

How the hell did that man manage to keep enough food around to feed everyone? she couldn't help wondering. It was like one of Aesop's fables come to life, the one about the bottomless pitcher of milk. No matter how many glasses were poured, the pitcher always remained full. In this case, it wasn't a pitcher, it was a bottomless refrigerator.

Someday she would have to ask Andrew about that.

* * *

There were two cars in Carole Stevens's driveway when Taylor pulled up twenty minutes later. Did the woman have company? she wondered as she parked her car at the curb.

Maybe it was a friend, offering condolences to the poor woman. Taylor was grateful that she wouldn't have to break the news to Eileen Stevens's mother about her daughter's murder. There was nothing worse than having to tell a parent that their child wasn't coming home again.

There should be a chaplain on the force who took care of that sort of thing. It was hard enough getting through each day alive, always running the risk of being shot—or worse.

Making her way up the front walk, Taylor took out her detective shield and ID. She held it up so that it would be the first thing that the woman would see.

There was a Christmas wreath on the door, in direct contrast to the sorrow that now resided within. Taylor rang the bell. It opened almost immediately.

"Mrs. Stevens?"

The question was merely for form's sake. The tall, thin woman who opened the front door was an older version of Eileen Stevens. And, eerily like Eileen, the light had been drained out of her eyes.

"Yes."

Taylor raised her shield slightly, calling attention to it. "I'm Detective McIntyre—"

"Yes, I know." It was then that the woman opened the door further, allowing Taylor to see that Carole Stevens wasn't alone. She had a six-foot-three guardian angel next to her. "Laredo told me you'd be coming."

Taylor's eyes shifted to Laredo, who smiled at her. She allowed her mouth to curve, but there was no humor in the expression.

"How thoughtful of him."

Laredo acted as if they'd just exchanged a hearty greeting. "Nice to see you again, Detective."

"I can't say the feeling is mutual," Taylor murmured under her breath. Eileen's mother didn't seem to hear her, but she was certain that Laredo did. His smile widened.

"Laredo is just here to support me," the woman told her, her voice echoing the hollowness that she obviously was feeling inside. Carole glanced at the man beside her and did her best to smile her gratitude. "Chet thought it might be a good idea."

Taylor looked from Laredo to the woman. Where'd she heard that name before? "Chet?"

"My grandfather," Laredo reminded her.

The man had a gift, she thought. Without uttering a single, derogatory word, he made her feel as if she were the intruder.

Taylor got down to business. "This isn't going to take long, Mrs. Stevens," she promised the woman, doing her best to cut Laredo out of the mix by turning her back toward him.

"I've got nothing but time," Carole told her sadly just before she turned on her heel to lead the way into the living room.

Mrs. Stevens sat down on the sofa, clasping her hands before her as if doing so would give her strength to get through this horrible ordeal. Laredo sat down beside her. Leaving Taylor to take a seat on the chair opposite the sofa. Again she felt isolated, like an outsider.

"I really don't know how I can help you," Carole confessed. "I don't know much about her life." It was obvious that the admission was painful for the woman. "Eileen and I just recently got back together again. She'd been angry at me for years, holding me responsible for nearly ruining her life." The sigh that escaped her lips was ragged. "Those were her words, not mine." Carole raised eyes that were bright with tears. "Do you have any children, Detective?"

The fact that Laredo eyed her with interest, waiting for her answer, didn't escape Taylor. "I'm not married."

A sad smile curved the thin lips as a faraway look came into Carole's eyes. "Neither was I."

Taylor caught the woman's point. She shook her head. "No, no children."

Carole nodded, as if she hadn't expected any other answer. "Then you have no idea how that can hurt, having your child hate you."

"Eileen didn't hate you, Carole," Laredo interrupted, his voice soft, kind, as he took the woman's hand and squeezed it, as if to give her support. "You made her take responsibility for her actions. You actually caused her to turn her life around and make something of herself. If anything, she should have been grateful to you."

Gratitude filled Carole's eyes. "I wish I could believe that, Laredo"

"Believe it," Laredo urged as if this was the one truth she could hang on to.

Rallying, Eileen's mother straightened, squaring her shoulders. She looked at Taylor as if she'd suddenly become aware of her presence. "I'm sorry. This is all still very new to me."

"I understand and I am sorry for your loss," Taylor told her with genuine feeling. No mother should have to outlive her child. She knew how devastated her own mother would have been if anything were to happen to any one of them.

Carole nodded. "Thank you." She took another bracing breath, then asked, "So, how can I help you?"

Taylor took a small, worn notebook out of her pocket. She'd thought to take it with her after writing down the woman's address.

"You can tell me about Eileen," she urged, watching the woman's face. Sometimes an expression said more than actual words did. "When the two of you got back together, did she say anything about being afraid of someone? About somebody bothering her or maybe sending her threatening letters?"

She had already asked the same questions of the victim's coworkers yesterday and gotten no feedback, but maybe Eileen had felt more at ease around her mother.

Carole shook her head. "Nothing. She never mentioned anything like that. All she talked about was her work. She was very excited about being made a partner."

"But?" Taylor let the word hang between them, picking it up from the tone of Carole's voice even though it hadn't been spoken out loud.

"But she didn't seem happy," Carole conceded. "Driven, but not happy. It was as if something was missing out of her life." At an apparent loss for words, Carole helplessly added, "Like everything she had just wasn't enough."

Funny that the woman had mentioned that. It was the exact same impression she'd come away with, walking around the victim's apartment last night.

Working with what Laredo had told her this morning, she tried to piece things together. "Your daughter got pregnant when she was seventeen and gave the baby up for adoption, didn't she?" Taylor asked Carole, approaching the sensitive subject slowly.

"Yes." Caution entered the woman's features. "What about it?"

Taylor knew she was grasping at straws, but sometimes that paid off. "Could Eileen possibly have been experiencing some remorse over that? Maybe feeling that she shouldn't have given the baby up?" As she spoke, ideas popped into her head. "Could your daughter perhaps have been considering trying to find her son after all these years?"

Carole almost laughed out loud. "Oh, God, no. When he was born, Eileen didn't even want to look at that poor child. I had second thoughts about giving him up, but she pitched a fit, insisting that if I kept him, she'd run away." Carole shrugged helplessly. "My first duty was to my daughter, so I let him go. Once she went off to college, I didn't see her anyway. I should have kept him," she whispered almost to herself, then roused herself and said with conviction, "No, Detective, I don't think she tried to get in contact with her son. Eileen never talked about him or the pregnancy. The second she left the hospital, it was behind her.

"My daughter didn't like children," Carole confided. "She never did. Thought that they were nothing but trouble." The woman's voice was sad as she continued. "I can show you her old room and pictures of Eileen when she was a little girl, but I really don't think any of that will help you."

Taylor never liked leaving any stone unturned. "You never know, Mrs. Stevens," she said encouragingly. "Sometimes it's the smallest thing that winds up solving a case."

A glimmer of hope passed over the woman's lined, concerned face. "I really hope so," she murmured, more to herself than to either one of the people in the room with her. Slightly unsteady, still dealing with the shock of the last twenty-four hours, Carole rose to her feet. Laredo was quick to take her arm and give her support. She smiled her gratitude. "You're a lot like your grandfather," she told him.

"I take that as the highest compliment, Mrs. Stevens," he replied.

Carole's eyes shifted toward Taylor. "This way," she urged, pointing down the hall to the back of the house before she walked in that direction.

Well, that was an hour of her life that she would never get back, Taylor thought after thanking Carole Stevens for her time and saying goodbye. There was no enlightenment to be garnered from her daughter's old room, other than the fact that in appearance, it was light-years away from the penthouse apartment that had seen the end of her life.

It was as if the two bedrooms had belonged to two very different people. The bedroom she'd just been in had, for all its disorganization, a kind of warmth to it that was glaringly missing from the one in the trendy, expensive penthouse. In the bedroom she'd just left there had been photographs pinned onto a bulletin board in a haphazard, overlapping fashion. The younger Eileen had had people in her life, friends she shared her time and her feelings with, not to mention the boyfriend who'd gotten her pregnant in the first place.

From all appearances, the successful Eileen slash murder victim had had only clients and acquaintances in her life. There was no evidence that she even *had* a personal life.

Did that mean something more than she was seeing? Was she missing something right there in front of her? In plain sight?

Taylor heard Carole saying goodbye again. Thinking the woman was calling out to her, she turned around only to realize that Carole wasn't talking to her, she was saying goodbye to Laredo. He was leaving, too.

Did he intend to follow her?

Instantly alert, Taylor waited until Carole closed the door, then went back up the walk to confront the not-so-private investigator.

"Just what exactly were you doing here?" she asked.

"Offering Mrs. Stevens some support," he answered amiably. "I thought we already cleared that up." And then he flashed that annoying smile of his, the one that seemed to wind itself like a corkscrew right into the center of her being. "You might not know this, but you do have a tendency to come on a little strong. I thought that I could act as a buffer for Carole if you got too carried away. After all, I was the one who told you where you could find her. If you rattled her, it would be my fault."

Taylor's eyes narrowed. "I don't appreciate being second-guessed."

"No guessing was involved," he countered. "I figured you'd come on like gangbusters. With me around, you didn't. Simple," he concluded.

"This might offend your ego, Laredo, but I don't temper the way I do things because you're around. And, now that I'm on the subject, I would really appreciate *not* having you around from now on." She pinned him with her eyes. "Agreed?"

The expression on his face told her that the answer to that was a resounding "No."

"Look, Detective McIntyre, it's a known fact that two heads are usually better than one. Why don't we just, off the record, join forces until we find out who killed Eileen Stevens? Think of the perks."

She refused to ask him what perks, fairly certain that he was going to say something about having him around for extracurricular activity should the desire hit.

"That way," he continued as if she'd asked him to elaborate, "you won't look so strange, talking to your-self. People'll think you're talking to me."

The man was a walking ego. "You think you're pretty clever, don't you?"

He lifted his shoulders in a casual shrug. "I have my

moments, but I'd rather think that I'm more intelligent than clever. How about it? Temporary partners? Off the record?" he pressed, extending his hand.

She looked down at his hand for a moment, then turned her back on it and him and returned to her car.

"I'll get back to you on that," was the last thing Taylor said before she got into the vehicle and pulled away.

"Yes, you will, Detective McIntyre," Laredo said to himself, watching her car make its way out of the development.

Chapter 5

Several hours later, after questioning more of Eileen Stevens's former clients and the people on the lower rung of her law firm, people who were more likely to pass on gossip, Taylor was no closer to solving the woman's murder than she had been before. Nobody loved the woman, but everyone respected her and felt she was an excellent lawyer. As far as she could determine there were no grudges, outstanding or otherwise.

Desperate for any kind of a decent lead, Taylor decided to return to the late lawyer's building. But this time, she wasn't going to wander around the tomblike apartment or talk to any of the woman's overly busy neighbors. Taylor wanted to question the security guard who had been on duty the evening Eileen had been murdered.

The young man, Nathan Miller, seemed surprised

to see her again. She'd already questioned the guard once and he had sworn that Eileen Stevens hadn't had any visitors. Anyone who didn't live in The Villas had to sign in and indicate who he or she was there to see. There'd been no name next to the dead lawyer's name.

"I'd really like to help you, Detective," Nathan told her with feeling. "But nobody went up to see her— unless they scaled the outside of the building," he added with an odd little smile, enjoying his own joke.

"What about the other residents?"

His forehead furrowed as if he was trying to make sense of her question. "You mean, did any of them go to see Ms. Stevens? I'd really have no way of knowing that. The residents get together all the time. That's why this place is so popular. We've got the fully stocked gym, the Olympic-sized pool, the—"

She held her hand up before Nathan could go, verbatim, through the features listed in the slick sales brochure. She'd already taken a copy with her and perused it. The Villas came across more like a spa slash mini-mall than a residence. From what she'd gathered from the neighbors, no one ever saw Eileen Stevens make use of any of the facilities she was paying so dearly for.

"No, what I want to know is did anyone come in to see any of the other residents that evening?" When the guard looked at her blankly, she elaborated. "A pizza delivery boy, a visitor you might not have recognized, a—"

Taylor knew that she was probably shadowboxing in the dark, but there had to be something. Someone had to have gotten to her. No way could Eileen Stevens have tied herself up like that.

Nathan shook his head to her suggestions and then abruptly stopped. "No, no—wait." His brown eyes widened as he looked at her.

She tried not to sound eager. "You remember something?"

"Yeah. There was somebody who came in, but he wasn't here for Ms. Stevens." Taking out the logbook housed on a shelf, he flipped back two pages. "Here it is," he read, then looked up, his hand spread out across the entry and holding down the page. "Mrs. Wallace had flowers delivered to her a little after seven."

Yes! "Did you see the delivery boy come back down?" Taylor pressed.

"No. But I was on my break," he explained quickly. Nathan looked crestfallen. "He could have left without me seeing him."

"You don't have security cameras?" Even as she asked, she looked toward the front doors.

"No. The residents consider it an invasion of privacy. I'm supposed to be enough," he added in a chagrined voice. "It's my fault, all my fault."

She felt sorry for him. He looked so young and inexperienced. Reality was taking a hard bite out of him. "Sometimes things happen that you just can't anticipate, Nathan," she told him. "Nothing's going to change if you beat yourself up over it. Do you know if Mrs. Wallace is in?"

He nodded his head. "She hasn't gone out on my shift," he told her.

He was qualifying his statements like a man who'd had his faith in himself shaken. "What floor is Mrs. Wallace on?"

"Second," he said with no hesitation. "But she's all the way over on the other end."

Taylor merely nodded. That didn't mean that the killer hadn't walked up one flight and then gone over to the dead lawyer's side. It *did* mean that a lot of planning had gone into Eileen Stevens's murder.

And she was still no closer to finding out why. Taylor banked down a wave of frustration as she went up to the other woman's apartment.

Dorothy Wallace was a widow in her late sixties who had a young woman's sparkle in her eyes. Dressed to show off all her best features—a body that was a combined product of religiously faithful workouts and the clever scalpel of a top plastic surgeon—Dorothy was just on her way out to meet "this young stud" for an early dinner "and 'whatever,'" she added with a broad smile.

Apologizing, Dorothy explained that she could only give her ten minutes because the "stud" apparently grew impatient when he was kept waiting.

"Flowers?" Dorothy repeated when the question of the delivery was put to her. Appearing perplexed, she slowly moved her head from side to side. "No, I didn't receive any flowers." A grin nothing short of wicked curved her carefully made up lips. "Not that night at any rate. I do get my share, though," she confided. "Don't you just love the old-fashioned type? The ones who know how to properly woo a woman?"

Now there was a word she hadn't heard lately, Taylor thought. Did anyone actually "woo" these days? She sincerely doubted it. Then she thought of Brian and her mother and decided to revise her conclusion, at least just a little. But outside of them, she was certain that men and women no longer had time for things like slow, languid courtships. Everything, including relationships—and breakups—seemed to occur in a hurry. Sometimes she had the feeling that life was almost over before it could even begin.

Philosophy aside, she had the answer she came for. Eileen Stevens's killer had gotten access to the building by posing as a delivery man for someone else.

After thanking the woman for her time, Taylor went back down to the ground floor. The security guard seemed impatient for her return.

"Well?" Nathan asked the moment the elevator doors opened.

Taylor shook her head. "Mrs. Wallace didn't receive any flowers."

"Oh, damn." He groaned as if he'd been physically punched in the stomach. "You mean that I let in the killer?"

"Maybe." She tempered her response only because he looked so terribly distraught. Taylor focused on the positive side. They finally had a lead. "Do you think that you could describe this guy to a sketch artist?"

"Maybe." Nathan thought a moment, then his head bobbed up and down. "Yeah, yeah I could," he decided. "Let me just call my boss and get someone to take my place. I can't just walk off my post."

"Except for breaks," she reminded him.

He slanted her a look she couldn't quite fathom. "Except for breaks," Nathan mumbled, sounding deeply ashamed.

Armed with the sketch of the so-called flower delivery man, Taylor returned to Eileen's firm.

The senior partner commented that he might have to put her on the payroll if she kept turning up. His one attempt at humor faded as he looked at the sketch and shook his head. He appeared genuinely disappointed when he told her that he'd never seen the man before. Neither had any of the other people at the law firm. No one she questioned even remotely recognized the man.

Five days into the murder and she felt as if she was banging her head against a wall. Still, for now this was her only lead and she wasn't about to give up on it.

She couldn't get over the feeling that she was missing a piece. Something that was out in plain sight and she just didn't see it.

It drove her crazy when, after several more days, her thoughts didn't gel. But neither did the feeling disappear.

"Try backing away from it," her older brother counseled. Zach had swung by her desk to ask if she wanted to grab some lunch. She'd been so preoccupied that she hadn't even heard him come up. He'd said her name twice before she even looked up. "Maybe it'll make more sense to you if you take a break."

Taylor laughed shortly. "The security guard at Stevens's building took a break and Eileen Stevens wound up dead."

Zach shook his head as he lowered himself into the

chair beside her desk. "Now you're just babbling. As your older brother, I'm telling you to come to lunch with me."

But she shook her head. "Sorry, I can't." She gestured at the empty desk that was butted up against hers in the cubicle. "Aaron's still away and I'm doing double duty."

Zach looked unimpressed. He knew the kind of workaholic his sister could be.

"So both of you need to eat. To keep your strength up and all that good stuff." As Taylor began to shake her head to turn him down again, he added, "Okay, as senior detective, I order you to come with me."

"Pulling rank?" she laughed.

He could remember when doing something like that would set her off. But they'd been kids at the time and squabbling had been a way of life. "If that's what it takes, you better believe it."

Taylor began to waver. Now that she thought of it, she could feel her stomach pinching. Had she had breakfast? She couldn't remember. She supposed nothing earthshaking would happen if she did stop to get something to eat.

And then it did.

"McIntyre," Lieutenant Harrigan called out, walking out of his glass-enclosed office. When both Zach and Taylor looked his way, he amended, "The pretty one."

"That would be me," Zach told her, rising. "Sorry, kid."

"Yeah, right." *Now what?* Taylor wondered, rising to her feet. "Yes, Lieutenant?"

The expression on the older man's face was stern. "You caught another one."

Confused, she looked at him blankly. "Another one what, sir?"

"Homicide." The single word hung in the air, lethal and treacherous.

She felt a little frayed around the edges. The last thing she needed was a new murder to pile onto the one she hadn't solved yet.

"No disrespect, Lieutenant, but aren't one of the other teams up?" She gestured vaguely around the room. Most of the desks were unoccupied, but that was only because the teams were out to lunch or in the field. "I'm still—"

Harrigan cut her short. "Same M.O. as your dead lawyer," he told her. "Hands and feet tied up and a leather strip around the neck, choking off the air supply."

Once was bizarre. Twice was eerily unbelievable. "You're kidding."

The lieutenant gave her a look that said she should know better. "When have you known me to kid?"

The flicker of hope died ignobly. "Right. Where's her body?" Taylor asked as she took her oversize, carry-everything purse out of the bottom drawer and slung it over her shoulder.

"His," Harrigan corrected. Both Zach and Taylor looked at him, obviously taken aback. "His body."

"His body?" Taylor repeated incredulously.

The barest hint of a smile came to the older man's lips. "Aced your hearing test, did you?"

Taylor blew out a frustrated breath. "So this wasn't personal, this is just some homicidal wacko getting his jollies."

"Draw no conclusion before its time," Harrigan advised. He handed her the slip of paper with the dead man's name and address on it. "Here you go. Dispatch just called."

"Terrance Crawford," she read out loud then saw the address. "Lakeview Middle School." She raised her eyes to the lieutenant's. "He's a teacher?"

"Not anymore," Harrigan contradicted with a heavy sigh.

"Okay, guess you're off the hook," Zach said to her as the lieutenant retreated to his office. "I'll take a rain check. But you get yourself something to eat, hear me?" She nodded dismissively, her mind already working on this newest twist. Was there a connection between the homicides, or was this killer just an opportunist? "If you're going to be the godmother of my kid," Zach told her as he began to walk away from her desk, "I want you healthy."

Taylor's thoughts vanished as her mind came to a skidding halt. She grabbed her brother's arm and turned him around to face her.

"Hold it!" she ordered. "What godmother? What kid?"

"You," he said in a mild tone, struggling to keep a straight face. "Mine."

"You don't have a kid." And then she backtracked. "Do you?"

Zach grinned. "According to Kasey, who's much more of an expert on these things than I am, considering she's a doctor, it's the size of a peanut. But it is mine. Ours," he amended with all the pride that flowed through a newly minted father's veins.

"Oh, God, Zach! A baby!" Excited, thrilled, Taylor threw her arms around her brother. There were a lot of babies of varying ages and sizes in the Cavanaugh family, but this was the first one for the McIntyre contingent. "Does Mom know?"

"Officially?" he asked, then shook his head as Taylor released her hold on him. "No. But she probably just heard you scream it out. Kasey and I thought we'd tell her and Brian over dinner tonight. Want to be there?" he offered.

Taylor knew her location tonight was still up in the air, depending on what she was going to learn at this new crime scene, but she said what was in her heart. "I'd love to."

Like the rest of them, including their mother, Zach had no illusions about the demands of the job. He read between the lines.

"I'll understand if you're not." He took his leave, saying, "Now go solve this damn thing before we have to set up another task force."

Taylor paused only long enough to kiss her brother, give him another warm, fierce hug, and then she rushed off. She had a body waiting for her.

It almost didn't seem right to feel this happy while going to investigate yet another murder but this ultimately kept them all going. The small, deep, unexpected pockets of happiness that they dipped into to sustain them.

Otherwise, it was all sorrow, all darkness in the worlds they occupied. She knew without exploring it that she wouldn't have been able to cope with that. Most likely, none of them could.

Thank God for her family. How would she have ever maintained her sanity without them? It was a rhetorical question.

Pulling up to Lakeview Middle School, Taylor parked her car right beside the patrol car and got out. It appeared to be the last parking space. The lot was completely filled with cars that undoubtedly belonged to the teachers who worked here.

Out of the corner of her eye she noticed one car parked off to the side that looked vaguely familiar, but then she shrugged it off. Lots of cars looked familiar at this point.

She wondered how the students were coping with this turn of events, or if somehow the teachers had managed to shelter them from the traumatic truth. The irony of the situation wasn't lost on her. This made twice. Two murders in two neighborhoods deemed exceedingly safe. Patrolmen were more likely to hand out tickets for failing to wear a bicycle helmet or not coming to a full stop at a stop sign than deal with the grisly details of a murder.

Walking up to the wood-framed double glass doors, Taylor took a breath and braced herself. She pulled open the right door with one hand, holding her badge in the other.

As she crossed the threshold, she found she didn't have to say anything. The principal, a Mrs. Hammond, was waiting for her and she pointed out the way as she fell into step beside her.

"I don't know what to say to the parents," Mrs. Hammond confessed, tension radiating from every pore as she obviously struggled to hang on to her composure. "Nothing like this has ever happened here before. Nothing," she repeated, her voice cracking.

"You need grief counselors," Taylor advised kindly. She paused for a moment, looking through her wallet. Finding the card she wanted, she handed it to the woman. "Call this number," she told her. "You'll get the help you need. Meanwhile, what can you tell me about the teacher who was killed?"

Mrs. Hammond swallowed before answering. "He didn't call in today."

Taylor looked at the stately woman, confused. "Excuse me?"

The principal ran her tongue quickly across her dry lips. "He wasn't here this morning and he didn't call in. I thought it was rather strange. He's one of our most dedicated teachers," she explained, her voice speeding up nervously with each word she uttered, her distress very evident. "He was always volunteering for after-school programs. The kids all love him. Loved him," she corrected. "And then, Jack opened up the closet where the equipment's stored—"

"Jack?" Taylor interrupted before the woman could continue.

But it wasn't the principal who answered her.

"The maintenance man," Taylor heard an all-too-familiar voice say.

No, it couldn't be.

But it was.

She didn't know which she was more, angry or stunned. "What the hell are you doing here, Laredo?" she demanded, swinging around to face him.

He appeared nothing if not easygoing as he answered, "Just lending a hand." Then, to placate her, he added, "I own a police scanner and heard the call being made to dispatch."

Trying to maintain her temper, Taylor turned to the principal.

"I'd like to talk to you later, Mrs. Hammond. Will you be in your office?"

"Yes." There was almost an echo in the woman's voice.

Taylor nodded. "Good. And please, make that call," Taylor pressed, indicating the card that she had just given her.

The principal glanced down at the card numbly, nodded and then retreated. She looked like someone on automatic pilot.

The moment the woman was out of earshot, Taylor whirled around to face the private investigator who was turning up more often than the proverbial bad penny.

"This is getting more than a little suspicious, Laredo."

He nodded, gazing down at the body that had fallen out of the closet at the frightened maintenance man's feet. "That's what I think, too."

She wasn't about to get sidetracked. Taylor pulled on his arm to get him to look at her. "I'm talking about you, turning up here and at the other crime scene—"

In a patient voice that instantly got under her skin, he reminded her, "I already told you what I was doing at the first scene. As for this one—" he looked back at the body again "—it's just too much of a coincidence not to be our boy."

He was really starting to tick her off. "*We* don't have a *boy*. *I* have a suspect."

He raised his eyes to hers, interested. "You do?"

He was making her trip over her own tongue. "I mean I would if I could find the guy who supposedly delivered flowers at the building the night Eileen Stevens was killed." To cover all bases, she'd spent the better part of one afternoon calling every florist within a twenty-mile radius. No one had a delivery scheduled to anyone at The Villas. She really hadn't expected them to.

"There was a delivery guy?" Laredo asked. "Who told you that?"

"The security guard. Nathan Miller," she added in case he'd talked to another one.

The information surprised him. "Funny, he never mentioned that to me when I talked to him."

"Maybe you're not as persuasive as you think," she couldn't resist saying.

"Maybe," he allowed. And then he smiled at her. "Maybe we could go out to dinner and you could teach me your persuasive ways."

Behind her, the patrolman who had been first on the scene and had called dispatch cleared his throat. "Um, Detective?"

Chagrined, Taylor turned toward the uniformed man. "Why didn't you run this man off?" she asked.

Nervous to be placed on the spot, the patrolman told her, "He said the Chief of D's would vouch for him."

"And you just took him at his word?" she asked incredulously.

"No, ma'am, I called in to check. And Chief Cavanaugh did. He vouched for him. And he told me to tell you that sometimes a little outside help is necessary."

Taylor rolled her eyes. Just what she needed. Her stepfather on this irritating man's side.

She didn't bother suppressing her deep-rooted sigh. Some days it just didn't pay to get out of bed. This was turning into one of those days.

Chapter 6

Taylor, grudgingly accepting Laredo's help, spent the better part of the afternoon interviewing everyone who was at the school when Terrance Crawford's body had been discovered. The primary question was: How did they feel about the dead teacher? The words the interviewees used might have varied, but the essence of what they had to say was the same: Terrance Crawford was a wonderful teacher who was loved by everyone.

Incredibly selfless, the science teacher slash coach gave of himself to the point of exhaustion. If there was an after-school program that needed someone to helm it, Crawford was the first—sometimes the only—one to volunteer his services. And if there was no funding available for the program, he found a way to run it for free.

It quickly became apparent to Taylor that, in his own

way, Crawford was as passionately devoted to his work as Eileen had been to hers. The difference being that there was no king's ransom to be had in the teacher's case. What Terrance Crawford reaped were not exorbitant fees but gratitude and accolades. As in Eileen's case, the main people in Crawford's world were his colleagues. The difference again was that, according to several teachers' testimonies, Crawford could kick back with them. Taylor sincerely doubted that Eileen had kicked back with anyone in years.

Because there were so many teachers, students and, in some cases, parents to interview, Taylor found herself having to reluctantly accept Laredo's help. Otherwise, there was no telling when she would finish and it would be a matter of the proverbial cutting off her nose to spite her face syndrome.

"Glad to see you're being sensible instead of territorial," Laredo had said when she'd relented and told him that he could talk to the teachers without her being present—as long as he showed her his notes afterward. "This way we can probably get the preliminary interviews done in one afternoon instead of two."

There was that *we* again, she thought as she herded off her group of teachers and students. Where did this man get off thinking they were a set? And just what was it about him that got her back up so fast? She was usually a lot more tolerant of people, even when they behaved like insufferable jerks. Since there was no answer, Taylor was forced to drop the matter. But it still gnawed away at her.

She was just getting to her last interview, the vice

principal, Alyce Chin, a diminutive woman who was particularly teary-eyed over Crawford's murder, when Taylor saw Laredo looking into the classroom through the glass window on the upper portion of the door.

Damn, she should have known that he would be finished first. But it wasn't a competition, right?

Doing her best to ignore the man's presence, which still felt intrusive despite the door that separated them, Taylor forced herself to focus on the gut feeling she had about the vice principal.

Alyce Chin wasn't telling her everything.

After getting the standard answers about how well liked the dead teacher had been, Taylor lowered her voice, making the exchange more intimate. "Were you and Terrance Crawford close?"

The young woman began to shrug, denial obviously rising to her lips. And then she sighed. The moment she did, she broke down.

Alyce's lower lip trembled as she hoarsely whispered, "Yes."

Taylor was not about to leave anything in an ambiguous state. She wanted everything to be perfectly clear and spelled out. "Does that mean you were seeing each other outside the school?"

The woman hesitated again, then answered, "Yes," in a small, lost voice.

Thank God, finally something personal. "Then what can you tell me about him?" Taylor pressed, trying not to sound too impatient or eager. "Did Terrance have any enemies, anyone he felt had it in for him?"

The vice principal's dark eyes widened in stunned surprise. "No, no, everyone loved him."

"Not everyone," Taylor reminded her. More tears slid down the other woman's cheeks. Taylor thought of Eileen and how the criminal lawyer had turned her life around after giving birth to her baby. "Was there something in his past that he was ashamed of? That might have come back to haunt him?"

Again Alyce Chin hesitated for a moment, as if debating over something. But then she shook her head. "No, nothing."

"You hesitated," Taylor seized on that, her eyes holding the other woman prisoner. "*Was* there something? Think, this is important, Alyce. It could lead us to whoever killed Terrance."

Loyally, the vice principal shook her head. "No." And then she pressed her lips together, testing the weight of her next words. With a reluctant sigh, she said, "This might be nothing…"

"Let me be the judge of that," Taylor coaxed.

"All right. Once, when he was over at my place and he'd had a few drinks, Terry told me that in his senior year in high school, he'd gotten a girl—another student—pregnant. When he found out her condition, he wanted to marry her. She called him an idiot and said that she wasn't about to compound her mistake by making an even bigger one. She gave the baby up for adoption even though he wanted to keep it. He offered to raise it, but she absolutely refused. It killed him that she could do that, that he had no rights as a father."

She shifted in her chair, uncomfortable about sharing

her late lover's secret. "I think that's why Terry got into teaching. He wanted to make up for not being there for his son. I know it sounds corny, but he wanted to make a difference, to touch as many young lives as he could."

From the first word of the narrative, Taylor felt her breath catch in her throat. Every nerve ending she had was now on high alert. If this was a coincidence, it was one hell of one.

"Did Terrance ever happen to mention the girl's name to you?" Taylor asked, mentally crossing her fingers.

Alyce thought for a moment, her expression indicating that she was having difficulty recalling. "Arlene, Irene, something like that…" Her voice trailed off as she searched for the name that sounded right.

"Could it possibly be Eileen?" Taylor asked.

The vice principal didn't answer immediately. Again her expression indicated that she was thinking. "Maybe. I really don't remember." Her shoulders slumped a little as she wiped away more tears. "I'm sorry. I just can't think right now."

Taylor's heart went out to the woman. How would she feel, losing someone she loved? Wasn't that why she shied away from relationships? Because giving your heart came with a high price tag?

"I understand," Taylor told her gently. "I gave your principal the name of a good grief counselor to call in for the students." Her mouth curved in a soft, sympathetic smile. "He works with adults, too."

Alyce pressed her lips together, nodding. She was struggling not to sob. "Thank you," she murmured.

Finished, Taylor had no choice but to go back into

the hallway—where Laredo was still lying in wait, she thought, bracing herself. Hopefully, he'd learned something useful, although she doubted he'd discovered anything as good as what she'd just gotten.

"That's one hell of a connection," Laredo said the moment she opened the door and walked out.

Taylor stared at him, dumbfounded. He couldn't possibly have heard. She'd had to lean in so that she could hear the vice principal herself.

"What is?" she asked cautiously.

"That the dead teacher is the father of Eileen Stevens's baby." This took the two murders in a whole different direction. He wasn't sure what that new direction was yet.

Her mouth almost dropped open. How did he know?

"You couldn't have possibly heard that," Taylor insisted.

"You're right," Laredo acknowledged. "I didn't 'hear' it. Technically, I read it."

Her eyebrows narrowed over the bridge of her nose. This was in print somewhere? How? "Where?"

"On Alyce Chin's lips."

Just who *was* this guy? "Now you're telling me you read lips?"

Laredo looked at her lips and that same annoying, utterly unsettling sexy smile slipped over his. The one that raised her body temperature by several degrees no matter how hard she tried not to let it affect her. "Yes."

"Is that part of your private-eye training?" she asked sarcastically.

"It's private investigator," he corrected. "And no, it's

not. My mother was hearing impaired. I thought walking a mile in her shoes would help me understand her better, understand what she had to go through every day. For the record," he added, "I also sign."

He also made her feel like an idiot, Taylor thought. She was shooting sarcastic remarks at him and he was telling her about being sensitive to his mother's disability.

"Anything else?" she asked in a flat voice.

Laredo shrugged, amused. "I figure the rest will come out as we go along."

"*We* are not 'going along.'" If he thought he could become her unofficial partner just because she let him question a few people, he was sadly mistaken. "You're only here because my stepfather seems to think that you could be an asset. Obviously, he's not always a very demanding person—"

"I bet you take care of that part for him," Laredo speculated. He saw her open her mouth and he rerouted the conversation before she had a chance to retort. "Why don't we get back to Eileen's mother and verify that the baby's father actually was Terrance Crawford?"

That had already crossed her mind, just not her tongue. "So now you're taking over the lead?" she asked.

Laredo raised his hands as if to surrender. He also attempted to harness his amusement—rather unsuccessfully, she noted. It still shone in the man's eyes.

"Just making helpful suggestions, Detective McIntyre."

She hated the way he emphasized her title. Hated having him hover around. Most of all, she hated that he seemed to always be right.

"If I want your 'helpful suggestions,' Laredo, I'll ask

for them." With that, she turned on her heel and walked down the hallway to the school's front doors.

She heard Laredo murmur, "No, you won't," under his breath behind her, but decided that there was no point in disputing that. After all, he was right. Again.

"Terrance Crawford?" Carole Stevens repeated the name they had put to her less than a half an hour later. "He was the father?"

"That's what we're asking you, Mrs. Stevens," Taylor said kindly.

They were in her kitchen, sitting at the table. Cups of tea Mrs. Stevens had poured cooled in front of them.

"I don't know," she admitted honestly, looking from one to the other. "I always thought it might have been, but you have to understand, back then there were always boys surrounding Eileen." A sad fondness came into her voice as she remembered. "She was like a little Scarlett O'Hara, stringing them all along. She loved the attention," Carole added needlessly.

"And she never confided in you?" Taylor asked. She thought of her own bond with her mother and felt grateful that there was absolutely nothing she couldn't come to Lila with.

An almost tortured laugh escaped the other woman's lips. "I was the last person Eileen would have confided in. Especially after I wouldn't let her have that abortion."

Nodding as if he understood, Laredo asked, "Did your daughter have any friends back then, someone she might have told about the baby's father?"

Carole thought for a moment, then rose to her feet. "Come with me."

She led them back to Eileen's room. Once there, she turned toward Laredo and pointed at the mattress. "Lift that, please. Eileen kept her phone book there, along with her diary," she explained. "For some reason, she thought I wouldn't catch on." Carole shook her head in disbelief. "Don't know who she thought changed her sheets once a week."

There were two small, five-by-six books, worn with time and the weight of the mattress, lying in the middle. One was a faded lavender, the other gray. Propping up the mattress with his shoulder, Laredo picked up the two books before she had a chance.

Damn but he was fast, she thought grudgingly. Laredo let the mattress drop into place.

Holding up the books, he asked Carole, "Mind if we take these with us?"

Carole locked her fingers together. It was obvious that until this moment, she hadn't even given either book a thought. Nor had she sought any comfort from flipping through the diary.

"If it'll help, take them." And then she hesitated. "I will get them back, won't I?"

"I guarantee it," Laredo promised, patting the woman's shoulder as he held the books against himself with his other hand.

"Give them to me," Taylor ordered the moment they were out of the house.

Not waiting for Laredo to hand the books over to her,

she laid claim to the gray bound address book and pulled it out of his hand.

"Yes, ma'am," he answered in a clipped, military voice, saluting her.

She ignored him and flipped through the book she'd secured. Only a few names were scattered through the pages.

All they needed was one, she thought as she drove back to the station house.

As she came to a skidding halt in the parking lot, she looked up into her rearview mirror. There was his car pulling into the lot right behind her. Getting rid of him was harder than exterminating an infestation of ants.

"We can divide the names up," he volunteered.

She stopped halfway up the stairs to the front doors. "Look, what will it take to get this through your head? You're a civilian."

"I know that," he responded amiably.

"And civilians don't work with cops on cases," she continued through gritted teeth.

"Sure they do. Happens all the time. Don't clench your teeth like that, Detective. It'll wear them away. You wouldn't like dentures," he assured her.

Taylor threw up her hands and ascended the rest of the stairs. She was using energy trying to ignore him when she should have been focusing on the case.

Laredo fell into step beside her.

As it turned out, of the few names in Eileen's old address book, only one person had not moved away. Valerie Ames still lived at the same address and had the same phone number as in high school. Valerie had never left her comfort zone. Twenty years after graduation, she still resided with her widowed mother.

Cautious at first, Valerie finally agreed to meet with them, but only in a public place. She chose a coffee shop not too far from her house.

"My mother still thinks she's entitled to know every little thing about me," Valerie complained in a voice that was almost painfully nasal, adding to its whiny quality. She tore open packet after packet of sweetener and poured the contents into her coffee container. "I swear that woman can hear things from the farthest room in the house."

Taylor didn't ask the logical question, if Valerie found living conditions so unpleasant, why didn't she just move out? She didn't ask because she didn't want to antagonize the woman or get drawn into a tedious discussion. All she wanted was an answer to one important question. Was Terrance Crawford the father of Eileen's baby?

"Terry Crawford?" Valerie repeated when the name was put to her. "Sure, he was the father of her baby. Eileen was crazy about him," she confided, then added, "for about three months. A record for Eileen." She made no effort to hide her snide tone. "But then she got pregnant and she was just angry all the time." Valerie paused to take a long sip of her coffee, then addressed her remark to Laredo, with whom, Taylor noticed, she was obviously flirting. "Especially at her mother."

"Because she wouldn't allow Eileen to have an abortion," Laredo said.

Valerie nodded, her chestnut hair bobbing up and down. "That was why."

Taylor cleared her throat. Valerie didn't look in her direction immediately. It was only when Laredo, his eyes on Valerie's, nodded toward her that the woman momentarily shifted her attention.

"We heard that Crawford wanted to raise the baby and was upset when he found out that he couldn't," Taylor said, leaving the statement open for comment.

Valerie shrugged her shoulders. "News to me, but then, Eileen didn't want to have the baby around. If Terry kept the baby, it'd be a constant reminder that she'd made a mistake. She popped that baby out and made sure that there was a social worker right there to whisk it away. Eileen was pretty organized for someone who was so messed up."

"She was messed up?" Taylor pressed.

Valerie nodded vigorously. "Hey, anyone missing a chance to play house with Terry Crawford had to have a few loose screws."

"Doesn't sound as if you and Eileen had much of a friendship," Taylor observed.

Valerie shrugged again as she drained her coffee container. "Hey, you make do." Setting the empty container down on the table, she rose. "Well, I've got to be getting back. Don't want to miss my program," she said cheerfully.

"Wouldn't want that to happen," Laredo agreed.

She paused for a moment at the entrance to the coffee shop. "Unless you'd like to ask me some more questions." Her words were directed at Laredo and it was obvious that questions weren't what she really had on her mind.

"Not right now," Taylor assured her. "But we have your number if anything new comes up."

Nodding, Valerie left.

"Think these murders have anything to do with the baby?" Taylor finally asked after a lengthy silence. They were on their way back to the precinct, where Laredo had left his car parked in the lot.

Laredo looked at her now, mildly surprised. "You're actually asking my opinion?"

"Right. What was I thinking?" Taylor shook her head. Maybe she was getting punchy. "Never mind."

"No, I'm flattered," he told her. "Surprised, but flattered."

"I don't want you flattered," she told him wearily. "I just want your take on this."

He'd been going over the situation in his head ever since they found out about Crawford's possible connection.

"On the surface, it looks as if it might have something to do with their past. The baby being the connection would be the logical conclusion, but not necessarily the only one." He laughed shortly. "I don't think this is Planned Parenthood taking drastic measures and striking back if that's what you mean."

"Never mind," Taylor repeated, this time with more feeling. Served her right for lowering her guard and thinking she could brainstorm with this man the way she had with Aaron.

"That, in case you didn't recognize it, was a joke," Laredo informed her patiently. "Loosen up, Detective

McIntyre." He leaned slightly forward in his seat, taking a closer look at her. "And stop frowning. Didn't your mother ever warn you that your face might freeze that way?"

She slanted a dismissive glance in his direction before taking a right turn. "My mother was too busy warning me about scruffy private investigators with big egos trying to horn their way in where they didn't belong."

Laredo nodded solemnly. "Smart lady." It was against his credo to say anything against anyone's mother, even in a joke. "I'll stay on the lookout for one and let you know if I see any."

"Another joke?" she asked warily.

"It's not a joke until you smile," he qualified, watching her.

Maybe he could take a light view of things, but she couldn't. "I've got some nutcase running around, tying wet strips of leather around people's necks and then watching them strangle to death. *And* I've got two dead people to account for. News flash—there's nothing to smile about."

He didn't see it that way. "There's always something to smile about, Detective McIntyre," he told her. "Sometimes you just have to look hard to find it, that's all."

She didn't agree, but she was in no mood to argue. "Right." Feeling suddenly drained, Taylor dragged her hand through her hair.

"Why don't I buy you dinner?" Laredo suggested out of the blue. She glanced quizzically in his direction. "Maybe things'll come together if you don't have to listen to your stomach complaining."

Now what the hell was he talking about? "My stomach?"

"Yeah. Can't you hear it?" He nodded toward it, as if she didn't know where to find it. "It's competing with your thought process—and mine."

Her thought process was being competed with all right, she thought. But it wasn't her stomach that was causing the problem.

Still, he did have one valid point. She *was* hungry. "All right, but you're buying."

"That's what I just suggested. Was I speaking too low for you?"

As a matter of fact, his voice *was* low. And it was getting to her in ways she definitely found distracting. "Shut up, Laredo. Nobody likes a wiseass."

She heard the smile in his voice. "I'll try to remember that."

She took the next turn a bit too sharply, struggling to bank down the unwanted reaction she was experiencing. "You do that."

Chapter 7

"So what do you do when you're not detecting, Detective McIntyre?" Laredo asked her as the waitress retreated with their orders.

When he'd offered to buy her dinner, Taylor had expected Laredo to bring her to one of the dozens of fast-food places that littered Aurora, serving anything from hamburgers to pizza to Asian food, all of which could be consumed on the run.

Instead, he'd brought her to Fiorello's, a well-reviewed, four-star restaurant that specialized in Italian cuisine. She'd always been very partial to Italian food.

Had this been just a lucky coincidence on his part, or had Laredo known about her preference? And if so, how? And why? Why was the private investigator trying to cull favor with her?

What was he up to?

"Your problem is that you overthink things," Frank had told her more than once. But then, little brothers had a tendency to be critical. It was due to the very nature of their position within the hierarchy of the family.

She supposed that maybe Frank had a point. It happened. After all, even a broken clock was dead-on twice a day.

"I sleep," she answered tersely. Before Laredo could say anything in response, she asked, "Do you come here often?"

"No." He took a sip of the ice water he'd requested. "As a matter of fact, it's my first time."

Well, at least he was being honest. So far. "What made you pick it?"

He looked at her for a long moment, as if weighing his answer. And then he laughed, shaking his head. "You don't stop."

That certainly wasn't an answer. Her eyes narrowed. "Excuse me?"

"Being Detective McIntyre. You really don't stop, do you? You just keep on 'detecting,'" he added when she continued to look puzzled.

He was trying to distract her. *I don't distract that easily, Laredo.* "Most people tend to go to a restaurant they're familiar with."

Their eyes locked. "There always has to be a first time."

He wasn't referring to going to a restaurant. As she had to consciously concentrate on breathing, she could feel his words slipping in under her skin, undulating their way through her whole frame. Settling into her very core. It took effort not to let her thoughts drift off.

"You *knew* I liked Italian food."

He'd asked Frank if his sister had any preferences when it came to eating out, but he wasn't quite ready to tell her that. Instead, he looked at her as if this was all news to him.

"You do?"

A two-year-old wouldn't have been fooled by this man, she thought. "You don't do innocent very convincingly, Laredo."

Broad shoulders lifted and fell in a casual shrug. "I guess I've got to practice in front of the mirror more often."

The conversation momentarily stopped as the waitress returned with their dinners. The young woman placed the Italian herb chicken before Laredo and the Alfredo shrimp with angel hair pasta in front of Taylor.

The moment the waitress backed away, Taylor leaned forward and said, "I'll take that as an admission."

She reminded him of a dog he'd once had. His grandfather had bought it for him, hoping that it would help him cope with the loss of his mother. Whenever the dog latched onto something, there was no way to get the animal to drop it.

"You must be hell on wheels in an interrogation room, Detective. I'd like to watch the next time you're up," he told her.

She couldn't decide if he was laughing at her or if he was serious. In any case, it didn't distract her from getting an answer to her question. "Why would you ask what my favorite food is?"

Waiting until after he sampled his dinner, Laredo countered with a question of his own. "Why wouldn't I?"

He was a master of the runaround. She would have expected nothing less. "I asked first."

Hungry, he took another bite of his food. He noted with satisfaction that despite her headstrong attack, Taylor was eating, too. "Maybe I'm just trying to find a way to soothe the savage beast."

"The expression is 'soothe the savage breast,'" she informed him, "and it refers to music, not food."

He paused long enough to grin at her. "Trust me, you wouldn't want to hear me sing."

Wasn't the man capable of a straight answer? If she did have him in an interrogation room, she had a feeling that he would drive her crazy.

"I've got a question for you," she posed gamely. "What do you do when you're not cracking wise?"

"I try to crack cases," he told her seriously. The next moment, the smile was back. Laredo leaned over the small table. Coming much too close to her. "Life's too short, Detective McIntyre. Have some fun with it before it's over." He indicated her meal. "Enjoy your food. Enjoy your diet soda," he added, lifting his glass in a mock salute.

Taylor left her glass where it was as she studied him. She was completely at a loss on how to read this man.

"Did you ask any other questions?" she asked. The query came out despite her resolve to drop the matter. But she suddenly had to know just how deeply he probed, how much he knew about her.

Something akin to goose bumps formed beneath the

sleeves of her jacket. There was no doubt about it, she thought darkly, the man stirred things up inside her.

She didn't *want* to be stirred. Not by someone so damn cocky and sure of himself.

"I ask lots of questions," he answered, again shrouding himself in pseudo innocence.

He knew damn well what she meant, Taylor thought. Although she was hungry, she hardly tasted the dinner she was eating.

"About me," she supplied tersely. "Questions about me."

"Oh, that. Well, yes I did." Without elaborating any further, which he had a hunch irritated her, he asked, "Did I break some kind of rule?"

She was very tempted to use the knife in her hand for something other than her dinner. "Why are you snooping around my life? You're supposedly here to investigate Eileen Stevens's murder."

"No *supposedly,*" Laredo corrected in all seriousness. He wound spaghetti around his fork like a pro as he spoke. "I *am* investigating her murder." That was a matter of honor, involving his word. "And yes, I am asking questions about you."

"Why?" she repeated.

Laredo put down his fork, his eyes on hers. He dropped his teasing tone. "Because I want to get to know you, Detective McIntyre. Because I'm attracted to you," he told her honestly, then added what she didn't want to hear. "And, unless my radar's completely off, I think that you're attracted to me, too."

No, no, she wasn't, Taylor thought fiercely. "Your

'radar' needs an overhaul," she informed him in a cool, dismissive voice.

When he looked at her like that, she felt as if he could see right through her. Right *into* her. Could see every thought she had. She knew that was absurd, and yet, she couldn't shake the feeling.

"Does it?" he asked quietly. "It's usually pretty accurate."

The only way she could save herself was if she got angry.

She got angry.

Of all the overbearing, pompous—

Words failed her, even in the deep recesses of her mind.

"Well, I'm sorry. Your 'radar' might be fine and dandy when it comes to the legions of other women in your life, but it shorted out when it came to me."

"There're no legions," he told her mildly, finishing his meal. "I was referring to the gut feelings I have when working a case." He smiled at her. "It's a general-purpose radar," he explained amiably. "Look, I'm used to putting my cards on the table. I don't want to make you uncomfortable."

Too late.

She took a deep breath, as if that somehow signaled a fresh start. "Fine, then let's just finish eating. I've got to be getting back."

Laredo looked at his watch. "It's after six. Aren't you supposed to be off duty by now?"

She worked a case until it was solved. Hours didn't matter. "Not while the case is open."

He watched her thoughtfully, trying to isolate what

it was about her that attracted him so. He couldn't pin-point it. She just did.

"You know," he told her, "even batteries need to get recharged. You've got to take a break sometime. What do you do for fun, Detective McIntyre?"

Her answer was automatic. "I put smart-mouthed private investigators in their place."

Laredo inclined his head indulgently. "What else do you do for fun?"

She didn't want him digging into her life, didn't want him trying to get close because she was afraid that he *would* get close. And that would be disastrous.

"Look, for some reason that escapes me, we're working a case together," she began, her voice strained. "I am not in the market for a new best friend—or anything else—so let's just keep this professional, okay?"

"Too bad. I could make a really good 'anything else,'" he told her teasingly.

Again, his smile slipped under her skin, all but fil-leting her.

And when he leaned over and slowly ran the back of his hand along her cheek, her heart went into double time, all but bursting out of her chest.

She pulled her head back. "That's not professional," she informed him in a voice that wasn't nearly as strong as she wanted it to be.

"Oh, I don't know. *Professional* means business," he told her, his eyes never leaving hers. "And I mean business."

Suddenly she didn't have enough saliva to swallow. "I've got to be getting back," she repeated. Somehow, she got her legs to work, her knees to lock so that they could support her. But as she began to rise, Laredo put his hand over hers.

He vacillated between being amused and being aroused. But whatever state he was in, he knew he was definitely intrigued. And curious. Very, very curious.

"What are you afraid of, Taylor?" he asked her in a low, silky tone.

He was using her first name again, making this feel oh so personal. She didn't want it to. Instinct told her that if she ventured forward, even a few steps, a trapdoor waited for her just up ahead. A trapdoor that would give way when she least expected it, causing her to plummet down to who knew where.

All she knew was that at the end, when she stopped falling, there would be pain. A great deal of pain. The best solution to avoiding pain was not to take that first step, especially not with someone like Laredo.

Someone who could, for reasons she couldn't begin to put into words yet, matter a great deal.

"I'm not afraid of anything," Taylor informed him with a toss of her head, rallying. And then she delivered what she hoped was the final, ego-shattering blow. "Except for maybe being bored."

It didn't have the hoped for effect. Taylor could swear she saw something enter his eyes. She'd seen it before. The look of a man rising to a challenge. And she had just issued it.

"Thank you for dinner," she said, her voice cold enough to freeze over a lake. She left the table—and him—quickly, without a backward glance.

Laredo didn't call out her name the way she'd expected him to. Didn't try to stop her.

Maybe she was rid of him, she thought, at least for the evening. Cheeks flushed as she made her way through the restaurant, she felt oddly feverish. Was that triumph? Or was it simply the result of being so close to him for the length of the dinner?

She didn't know, didn't care, Taylor told herself. All she wanted was to be in her car, driving away from here—and Laredo.

Though she loathed to admit it, the damn, irritating man was right. It *was* past her shift and maybe, just for tonight, she'd go home to ponder over the notes she'd taken and to backtrack over things. Maybe while doing that, she'd find something that would help her untangle these two murders.

Having Laredo hovering around her definitely did mess with her thinking process and she didn't need that. Didn't need a tall, dark, handsome man watching her as if he knew what made her tick—as if he knew what she wanted.

How could he when she didn't know herself? she thought, pushing open the front door and hurrying out of the restaurant.

The breeze that greeted her was a cool one, stinging her heated cheeks. The air was moist and heavy with humidity. Winter was California's rainy season. That was all she need now, rain. Everything seemed to be working against her.

For a moment, she tried to get her bearings, scanning the area for her car. As she stood there, Taylor thought she heard someone coming up behind her. She heard the footsteps half a second before her name was called.

"McIntyre."

She would have swung around on her own, but she never got the chance. The person who'd called out to her caught her arm and did it for her, bringing her around to face him one shaky heartbeat before he pulled her into his arms and brought his mouth down to hers.

If asked, Laredo wouldn't have been able to say just what had come over him. Despite the image he projected, he wasn't the kind who let impulse rule him. At least, not usually.

This time was different.

This time, there had been an almost insatiable need to satisfy his curiosity. To satisfy a strange hunger he had never encountered before. Somewhere deep in his soul, he knew she'd forgive him.

But if he didn't find out what her lips tasted like, he would never forgive himself.

Besides, he had something to prove.

Self-defense reflexes were as automatic to her as breathing. Or, at least, they had been. But they failed her now, freezing and breaking up like so many brittle shards of glass. They might have been as automatic as breathing, but then, she wasn't really breathing, either. Her breath had backed up in her lungs.

Taylor found herself spinning off into a place where neither time nor space played a part. She was only aware of a tremendous wave of heat, beginning in the distance and then suddenly, like a back draft, whooshing over her.

Consuming her.

Making her knees and torso feel so weak that they barely supported her. It took every fiber in her being not to embarrass herself by sinking down to the ground.

But she was certainly sinking into something far greater than she was. If she didn't act, it would overpower her.

Vaguely, the thought occurred to Taylor that she should be angry at Laredo. She should be pushing this egomaniac away with both hands.

And yet, she couldn't.

Didn't want to.

Instead, she wound her arms around his neck and brought her body in closer to his. She could feel the very blood rushing in her veins. Could feel every single rock-hard ridge of Laredo's frame against hers.

Adrenaline raced through her, heightening what she was feeling.

The fact that she was aware of his arms closing around her, of his mouth working nothing short of magic over hers, only deepened her pleasure rather than ignited her indignation.

What the hell was wrong with her? Why was she enjoying this? Didn't she realize that he was pleasuring himself at her expense?

Why wasn't she angry?

Because she was too swept away. And enjoying this far too much.

Somewhere in the back of her mind, Taylor was conscious of the restaurant door opening and then closing again. Of people—a couple—sidestepping them as they left Fiorello's.

Were they staring at them? She didn't know. Didn't

care. All she wanted was for this delicious sensation to continue.

And then it stopped. Just like that, there was space between her lips and his. The contact, the almost spiritual binding of souls, was suddenly broken.

She only realized that her eyes were shut when she had to open them. At the same moment, she heard Laredo say, "Wow."

Had she possessed the strength, she would have pulled back her hand and slapped him. But as it was, her arms hung almost limply at her sides.

Useless.

At least he wasn't smirking.

"You certainly pack some kind of a wallop, Detective McIntyre," Laredo murmured as his eyes swept over her face. There was something different in his voice, something she couldn't identify. "Maybe I should be the one who's afraid."

She cleared her throat, hoping that she wouldn't squeak when she spoke.

"Maybe you should be," she agreed.

"Would it be too presumptuous if I assumed that you weren't bored?"

She stared at him, trying to process what he was asking. Her mind was as numb as her body was not. "What?"

"Bored," he repeated. "Back in the restaurant, you said you were afraid of being bored. You didn't act as if you were bored, but I've learned never to take anything for granted."

Bored? Ecstatic, delirious, excited beyond belief, yes. Definitely not bored.

But she would die before she admitted it. She wasn't in the business of feeding egos and his, she was certain, was large enough.

"Maybe you should learn not to ask so many questions," she told him, turning her back on Laredo and beginning to walk away.

"Can't," he called after her. For the time being, he let her go. He needed time to himself to process what had just happened. "It's the nature of my job."

"See you tomorrow, Laredo," she said without turning around.

"Count on it."

That, she thought, was just the problem.

What she needed, Taylor told herself as she got in behind the steering wheel of her vehicle, was a cold shower and a hot drink. Preferably something to knock her out. And to erase the lingering effects of his mouth on hers.

She wondered if there was an eraser large enough.

Chapter 8

"Something wrong, Johnny?" was the first thing Chester Laredo asked when he opened his front door that evening.

As tall as his grandson and almost as muscular and trim, Chet Laredo had the same bright blue eyes and he sported an identical full head of hair, although his was a mixture of black and gray with just a little white weaving through.

He stepped back now, allowing Laredo to enter, studying his grandson carefully. There was something different about him tonight, but he couldn't quite put his finger on it.

In his seventies, Chet had worked for all of his adult life, but he had never been one of those people, no matter where his work took him, who'd been too busy for his family. Johnny's welfare always had top priority over everything else and he'd lived his life accordingly.

The aroma of something tasty and familiar wafted from the kitchen. No matter where he traveled, this would always be home to him, Laredo thought fondly. More accurately, the man he'd stopped by to see would always be home to him.

Comfortably planting himself on the sofa, Laredo looked up at the older man. His grandfather was studying him. *You can take the man out of the CIA, but you can't take the CIA out of the man,* he thought, amused.

"Does something have to be wrong for a grandson to stop by to see the crusty old man who raised him?" Laredo asked innocently.

About to lower himself into the richly padded armchair adjacent to the sofa, Chet pretended to scowl.

"Hey, watch that 'old' stuff, boy," Chet warned. "I can still take you, you know." And then he added with a fond smile, "Just not with one hand tied behind my back anymore."

"Take me?" Laredo questioned.

"Yup." Reaching for his remote, Chet shut off the early news program he'd been watching off and on for the last hour. "I still have a few moves up my sleeve."

Laredo laughed. "I thought you taught me everything you knew."

A look that could only be described as wicked amusement slipped over the older man's features. "Not everything, Johnny. Some things I kept back for a later date. A man always wants to be useful to his family."

Laredo smiled at that. He couldn't help thinking how

very different his life would have turned out had his father's father not been there for him. Chet had taken both him and his mother in when his father, Bret, a Navy SEAL, was killed on a mission whose exact details he would probably never learn. And then, several years later, his mother had died in a car accident. Laredo knew he would have been deemed an orphan and absorbed by the system had it not been for his grandfather's very large heart.

There were no words to describe how grateful he was—and always would be—to his grandfather.

"I think you went way beyond 'useful' a long time ago, Chet."

Chet smiled, both at the compliment and at the fact that his grandson remembered to address him by his first name. "Grandpa" had always made him feel as if he were being put out to pasture prematurely, something he'd vowed a long time ago would never happen.

That was the reason why he'd taken himself off the active roster at the CIA and opened up his own security firm a little more than five years ago. He firmly believed that work, the right kind of work, kept a man vital.

So did the right kind of woman. He'd shared both thoughts with his grandson more than once, especially the latter. It pained Chet that while his own son had been married and a father at Johnny's age, Johnny was still very much unattached—and appeared to be content to remain that way.

Though he didn't say it, he wanted to bounce his great-grandchild on his knee before he was dispatched on his final mission.

"Flattery will get you nowhere, boy." Piercing blue

eyes narrowed as Chet looked at his grandson. "And it won't distract me. Now, I repeat, is there something wrong?"

There were times Laredo could *swear* his grandfather was clairvoyant. But he kept a poker face as he said, "Why would you ask?"

Chet leaned over the arm of his chair, moving a shade closer to his grandson. "Because you look like something's just rattled the foundations of your world."

Laredo shook his head. "Nope, foundations are just fine and unrattled." Quickly, he changed the subject. Chet had a way of being able to delve right into his head and he really didn't want to talk about Taylor and what had happened outside the restaurant. "Look, I stopped by to let you know that your girlfriend's daughter's murder might not be an isolated incident after all."

That surprised Chet. He slid to the edge of the armchair. Johnny had his attention. "What do you mean by that?"

"There was another murder today." Laredo was surprised that the TV stations weren't carrying the story yet. "A middle-school teacher. They found him in the supply closet. Whoever killed him used the same M.O. that Eileen's killer had."

"You mean there's a serial killer running loose?" Chet asked. Serial killers were not as uncommon as the public might think. It just took the right detective to make the connection between crimes. Being able to share information made the discovery that much easier.

Laredo spread his hands. As far as he knew, the verdict was still out on that. It could just be one person, enamored with a certain method, seeking revenge against a couple of people.

"Maybe, maybe not."

Chet snorted. Some of the tension left his shoulders. "Just like your father. Double-talk. Talk straight, Johnny," he ordered. "If the M.O. is the same for both murders, why wouldn't you think it was the work of a serial killer?"

"Because the two victims had a connection."

A familiar, keen look entered his grandfather's blue eyes. Laredo knew that his grandfather absorbed every word, every nuance and that his mind was factoring it all in.

"A connection? What was it?" Chet prodded.

"Seems that the dead teacher got Eileen Stevens pregnant when they were both in high school."

Chet whistled softly to himself. "Damn, life certainly has a way of surprising you."

The observation had Laredo's thoughts immediately shifting to Taylor. There was no denying that he'd surprised himself when he had kissed her. He'd been even more surprised by his reaction to that simplest of intimate acts. The woman had damn near curled his toes and that didn't happen easily. Or often. Laredo wasn't altogether certain he liked that.

"Yeah, it does."

Chet watched him for a long moment, as if plucking thoughts out of his grandson's head. "You're not talking about the case, are you?"

"Sure I am, Chet." Laredo's tone was deliberately light. "You know, Carole Stevens isn't a bad-looking lady."

"No, she's not," Chet wholeheartedly agreed, allowing Laredo to change the topic.

Laredo had never known his grandmother, other than through photographs. Michelle Laredo had died before he was born. His grandfather could stand a little female companionship in his later years.

"Maybe you could offer her a shoulder to lean on," Laredo suggested.

"Been thinking about it," his grandfather admitted, nodding his head.

"Maybe you should do more than just think," Laredo coaxed.

Chet laughed. It was a rounded, full-bodied sound. "Since when have you decided to play Cupid?" Chet asked. "Seems to me that I haven't seen a lady on your arm for way too long."

Laredo grinned. "I've been busy. Besides, I wouldn't bring them around where an old fox like you could steal them away from me."

Chet doubted that anyone could steal the woman his grandson set his mind to.

"Steal them?" Chet echoed. "Hell, I'd be too happy to see you finally settling down to do anything except hit my knees and give up a prayer of thanksgiving." He eyed Laredo "That going to be happening anytime soon?" his grandfather asked.

"Hitting your knees and praying?" Laredo asked innocently. "I'd say that was entirely up to you, Chet." He took pity on the man and added, "As for the other part, I'll get back to you on that."

"You do that, Johnny." The subject, he knew, was

closed. For now. Chet rose to his feet. "I was just going to sit down and have some dinner. Join me?"

"I already ate. But I can keep you company," Laredo offered.

Chet smiled and slipped an arm around his grandson's shoulders as they both walked into the kitchen. "I'd like that."

Taylor usually slept like a rock. The minute her head hit the pillow, she was out. Zach had once speculated that she could probably fall asleep hanging from a hook in the closet. When she was tired, nothing got in the way of her getting a good night's sleep.

Nothing but the unnerving memory of J. C. Laredo's mouth and the magic it effortlessly wove as it passed over her own.

When she went to bed, Taylor was exhausted, but it didn't matter. Sleep had gone off on a holiday without any warning or forwarding address, leaving her tossing and turning. Every fiber of her being insisted on reliving those few moments in front of the restaurant, when time and the world had stood still and someone had turned up an inferno.

Questions popped up in her head. Questions that would never receive any answers because there was no scenario that would lead to her making love with the tall, sexy private investigator. God knew that she was not about to feed Laredo's ego or blunder into a situation she had no experience with.

There'd never been a man in her life she'd even remotely wanted to plan a future with, or even make love with. And Laredo would probably recoil in horror if he knew she was a virgin.

Besides, she was certain that the longing she felt would bring nothing but disappointment because, in her experience, her imagination was far more satisfying than anything reality had to offer. Turning on her side again, Taylor punched her pillow, vainly trying to find a soothing, comfortable place for herself. There just wasn't any to be found tonight.

Damn the man and his lethal mouth anyway.

She needed all her faculties in top running order, not feeling as if she'd been used to wipe the floor. If she didn't get some sleep soon, she would be a zombie come morning.

Another hour passed and she was still doing a human imitation of a spinning top. Desperate, Taylor got up and went to her medicine cabinet. A couple minutes of rummaging around and she found what she was looking for. It was one of those nighttime headache remedies that tacked the letters *P.M.* to the end of its brand name. She'd picked it up in the store a couple of months ago by mistake, then decided there was no harm in keeping the pills until their expiration date came up. "Just in case."

"Just in case" had arrived.

Resigned, Taylor popped one pill into her mouth, swallowing it without water, an ability that always made her sister shiver when she saw her do it. Hoping that would do the trick, Taylor went back to bed.

Lying down, she willed the over-the-counter medication to work.

* * *

Taylor had no idea what time she dropped off to sleep. All she knew was that when she finally woke up, early sunlight was shining into her bedroom and she felt as if someone had run her over with a double-coupled semi. Twice.

She was also running late. She should have already *been* at work, not getting ready for it.

"Damn, damn, damn."

Bolting out of bed, Taylor hurried into her shower. She was about to turn on the water when she looked down and saw that she was still wearing the jersey she used as a nightgown. Talk about being out of it. No more sleep remedies for her.

"Get with it, McIntyre," she ordered sternly.

Peeling off the jersey, Taylor hurled it onto the floor outside the shower. She turned the cold water on and let it blast her in an effort to get into gear. But she hadn't counted on it to rival the temperature of ice cubes.

A screech sounding not unlike a tortured cat escaped her lips as she quickly grasped the faucet and moved it toward a less-than-subzero setting.

She was just beginning to breathe normally again when she thought she heard a door banging open.

Her door?

Before the thought could actually register, Taylor saw the outline of someone through the frosted glass.

Someone who was running into her bathroom.

The only weapon that was available was the long-handled scrub brush. Better than nothing. She grabbed it just as the shower door was being yanked open.

Outrage flooded through her when she saw who it was. Laredo!

"Are you all right?"

The question, begun in concern, drifted away as the sight of her imprinted itself on his brain. Belatedly, he jerked his eyes back up to her face.

Embarrassed, furious, words failed her. Taylor grabbed the shower door and pulled it out of Laredo's hand, slamming it so hard it popped open again. She bit off a curse as she closed it a second time.

He'd gone too far this time, she thought, outraged.

"What the hell do you think you're doing?" she sputtered.

She heard him answer his own question before he addressed hers.

"I guess you are all right." And then he apologized. "Sorry, I heard you scream and I thought you were in trouble."

"I didn't scream, I gasped," she corrected angrily. "Don't you know the difference? The water was cold. And what are you doing here, anyway?" How much longer did she have to put up with Laredo popping up where he didn't belong?

"Looking for you," Laredo answered simply. His back to the shower stall, he addressed his words to the opposite wall. "I called the precinct, but they said you hadn't come in yet. So I thought I'd swing by your place to see if you'd left yet. When I saw your car parked in your space, I thought maybe you were running late for some reason."

That still didn't answer her question. "Why are you

here?" Taylor enunciated each word with barely suppressed anger.

He had her trapped, she thought. There was no way she could keep her dignity and still step out to get her towel. She stared at the back of Laredo's head. If he turned around, she was going to have him drawn and quartered.

"Hand me that towel that's hanging on the rack," she instructed. "And keep your eyes forward."

There was no missing the warning note in her voice. Laredo took the towel and, still averting his eyes, held it out to her. He felt her grabbing the towel out of his hand, heard her yanking it through the small opening she'd allowed between the frosted door and the shower frame. When he heard the door being shut again, he moved back to the spot where he'd been standing and resumed staring at the opposite wall.

"I didn't mean to startle you," he told her by way of an apology.

She didn't answer.

Wrapping the towel tightly around herself, Taylor secured it. The realization that it was a little like closing the barn door after the horse had run away didn't escape her. She was certain Laredo had gotten more than just a fleeting glimpse of her naked body when he'd yanked the door open.

"I'm waiting," Taylor announced as she opened the door and stepped out of the shower stall.

Very cautiously, he turned around until he was facing her. Damn, but she looked sexy, he couldn't help thinking. Even with dripping hair and no makeup. But, sexy or not, he had no idea what she was talking about.

"For…?" he asked, leaving the rest of it up in the air.

In a perfect world, her answer would somehow dove-tail with the sensations and blatant desires now charging madly throughout his system, threatening to overwhelm him if he lowered his guard. With very little encourage-ment, he would have gladly yanked the damp towel away from her body and set about pleasuring them both. Her first because he knew she had to be won over. But, in doing that, in pleasing her, he would also accomplish bringing pleasure to himself.

Laredo cleared his throat as he struggled to get his mind back on the right track. It took a surprising amount of effort.

The reason why he'd come looking for her in the first place was all but forgotten in the wake of the reason he wanted to be here now. He wanted her. Wanted her in every damn sense of the word, Laredo thought as itches that he wasn't at liberty to scratch ran rampant through him.

Suddenly warmer than she knew the room tempera-ture warranted, Taylor felt incredibly vulnerable. She absolutely hated that.

"I'm waiting for you to tell me why you came looking for me," she choked out. He had no right to be here, shaking her up like this, no right at all.

It took Laredo a second to actually remember what had originally brought him here. "I had an idea."

She'd thought he'd burst in because of something big, like—God forbid—another body being found. Taylor blew out a breath. "I will alert the media, but first, get the hell out of my bedroom," she ordered, walking past him as she crossed from the bathroom to her bedroom. She had to get dressed and she wasn't about to do it with Laredo standing in the room. With her luck, he probably had eyes in the back of his head.

Laredo gave her no argument. He stepped out into the tiny hallway that led from her bedroom into the living room. The second he crossed the threshold, the door behind him slammed shut. It barely missed hitting him in the butt.

"I could have you arrested, you know," she informed him, raising her voice so that it carried through the closed door. Quickly, she hurried into her clothes. "For breaking and entering," she elaborated in case the charges escaped him.

"I had probable cause," he countered. "I heard you scream."

She laughed shortly. "And you were coming to my rescue."

"Yeah, I was."

Finished dressing, Taylor sighed at the answer, then opened the door. Maybe he was telling the truth. Besides, she didn't have time to waste having him booked, even though the idea was more than a little tempting.

"Okay," she told him, walking out holding a pair of shoes in her hand. She dropped them on the floor and then stepped into them. "We'll let it go for now." Adjusting the back of one shoe, she looked at him. "What's this big idea you couldn't wait to share?"

"I don't know how big it is," he prefaced, "but I thought we could take a picture of Crawford and show it to that security guard in Eileen's building. Who knows, maybe Crawford paid her a visit or two and that set off a chain of events."

Offhand, she didn't see how they could follow that up, seeing as how both participants were dead, but stranger things had happened.

After rolling the suggestion over in her head, she shrugged. "Can't hurt, I suppose."

All things considered, the idea wasn't half-bad, but she wasn't about to admit that to him. Not just yet, anyway. She was still trying to come to terms with the fact that he had seen her naked. She knew he had despite the fact that he had been quick to avert his eyes and she had yanked the door out of his hands at lightning speed. There had been a split second. She had almost *felt* his eyes slide over her. Maybe not at length, but still thoroughly.

"Nope," he agreed, "can't hurt—and it might just lead us somewhere." Anything was better than just sitting around, twiddling his thumbs and reviewing notes he'd already committed to memory.

"Maybe," she allowed without feeling. Taylor twisted her still-damp hair into a knot and then secured it with a couple of pins.

He looked at her more closely. "You look a little tired, Detective McIntyre. Up all night working the case?" he guessed.

No, up trying to work you out of my mind. "Something like that," she answered.

"We can stop for breakfast if you want," he offered, following her out of the apartment. "Orange juice might perk you up. I can drive so that you don't run the risk of falling asleep behind the wheel."

If he was trying to ingratiate himself with her, the man was wasting his time. "I don't eat breakfast and I am more than capable of driving my own car," she informed him tersely.

"Shouldn't skip breakfast," he told her cheerfully. "Most important meal of the day."

"So Andrew Cavanaugh likes to say," she murmured under her breath.

"Wise man."

"Yes, he is. You, however, are an annoying man—and on borrowed time," she underscored.

"I grow on people," he assured her.

"So does fungus," she pointed out. "That doesn't exactly make it something to look forward to."

"We're definitely stopping for coffee," he informed her with finality.

Chapter 9

After stopping at the precinct in order to pick up the best photograph from the ones that had been taken of Terrance Crawford at the crime scene, Laredo and Taylor went to see the security guard at Eileen Stevens's building. Taylor insisted on using separate cars.

"I'm beginning to think you don't like my company, Detective McIntyre," Laredo observed when she told him she intended to go in her own car—and he was welcome to follow in his if he wanted.

She smiled, but just barely. "I guess you really *are* astute, Laredo."

"And you, Detective McIntyre, are one tough lady." He noticed that his observation pleased her.

Pressing a button, Laredo released the security

system in his vehicle. It beeped twice in response as all four locks popped open.

"As long as you know," Taylor replied, getting into her car.

Even though he knew the way, Laredo opted to follow behind her. As it turned out, if he hadn't, he would have missed her vehicle suddenly veering off the given course. He watched in surprise as she drove off in an entirely different direction.

What was going on here?

Taking care not to lose sight of her car, Laredo flipped open his cell phone. Eyes on the road, he pressed the number 9, which was the key he had assigned to her cell phone when he'd programmed it in the other day.

The phone rang three times before she answered.

"Trying to ditch me, Detective?" he asked.

Up ahead, he saw her make a sharp right. His was wider as he pushed down on the accelerator, determined not to lose her.

Taylor glanced up into her rearview mirror and saw him narrowly avoid fishtailing. "No, but I can give you a ticket for talking on your cell phone while driving."

"Police business," he pointed out. It was one of the exceptions to the ruling that had recently been passed against cell phone usage in cars. "Besides, I'm using a speakerphone. You can save your ticket, Detective. I've got both hands on the wheel." He heard her sigh and smiled to himself. "By the way, I thought you said we were going to The Villas."

"We were, but that'll have to wait. I just got a call."

He didn't have to guess what the call entailed. Her lieutenant wouldn't have abruptly rerouted her to an entirely different case. That meant that another body, sporting a leather choker, had turned up to be added to the list.

This was getting put of hand. "You're kidding."

"I only wish," she said with feeling, watching the road for the next turn. "Dispatch just got a call that two patrolmen found another body. This time it was in an alley."

He shared her feeling of disbelief. "The same M.O. as the others?"

"Same M.O. And it gets better," she added wearily. This newest development tended to blow the other theories out of the water. "This time, the victim is a homeless man."

She heard Laredo whistle softly under his breath. "Sounds like we really do have a serial killer on our hands," he speculated.

On the outside, yes, but she still harbored doubts. But for now, she'd agree with him. "Looks like it."

Laredo watched as the vehicle in front of him turned right at the next corner. He followed suit. "You don't sound convinced."

The way he could crawl into her head made her uneasy. What else could he intuit? "Could have been done to throw us off," she speculated. "The killer obviously has no problem taking a life. Who better to kill for the purposes of camouflage than some homeless man nobody is going to miss?"

There was silence on the other end, as if he was thinking. She didn't have time for this. But just as she was about to close the phone, he spoke up. "You've got a point, Detective McIntyre."

Detective McIntyre. His usage of her title and last name in almost every other sentence got on her nerves. It was formal and there was nothing formal about him. Besides, he'd kissed her and burst into her bathroom while she was taking a shower. The damn man had seen her naked. Somehow, calling her "Detective" with every other breath felt as if the private investigator was mocking her.

"You can call me Taylor."

"Thank you, Detective McIntyre." Laredo didn't bother keeping the grin out of his voice. In response, he heard the *click* of her phone as she terminated the call.

No two ways about it, he thought, tucking his phone back into his pocket, she was definitely one fascinating woman.

Taylor rocked back on her heels as she studied the dead man on the ground, trying not to let the stench of his body overwhelm her.

It was a homeless man, all right. And he had been murdered in the same fashion as the lawyer and the teacher before him had. The man, roughly in his mid-fifties she judged, had had his hands and feet bound, with duct tape over his mouth and a piece of leather stretched to the limit around his neck.

Taylor didn't need a coroner to tell her that the man had died from strangulation. The ventricular hemorrhaging in his eyes told her that.

A thorough search performed by the younger of the two patrolmen showed that the man had no identification on him.

Rising, Taylor dusted off her knees. "Tell the M.E. I want this man fingerprinted. Maybe we'll get lucky and he served in the military or held down a government job—"

"Or served time," Laredo interjected.

"Yes, there's that, too." At the very least, she could hope that the man'd held a California license in the last ten years. Thumbprints were required and all it took was one match to tell them who this latest victim was. She didn't like the fact that he was anonymous. What if he was the key to it all?

She heard the coroner's van pulling up into the alley. Taylor stepped back to give the attendants who emerged from the vehicle room to work. As she watched, trying to make sense of this latest development, the attendants bagged the body, placed it on the gurney and then withdrew.

That was when she saw it. There was a card on the ground. It had been missed because it had fallen beneath the body.

Was that deliberate? she wondered, taking out a handkerchief. She used it to pick up the card.

"I need to bag this," she told the closest crime scene investigator. The man took a plastic bag out of his case and handed it to her. Taylor slipped the card inside very carefully, sealed the opening and then studied it.

"It's a mass card," Laredo observed, looking over her shoulder.

"I know what it is," she told him. She flipped the card onto its face. There was a picture of St. Thomas More on the other side. "There's a saint you don't see every day," she murmured more to herself than to him.

"The card there by accident?" Laredo voiced the question that was on her mind as well. "Or is the killer trying to tell us something?"

If that was the intent behind leaving the mass card beneath the murder victim's body, a multitude of questions began to spring up in her head.

"Why now?" she asked. "Why with the third victim and not the other two?"

Laredo shrugged. "I guess we're going to have to catch him before we find that part out."

Very carefully, she slipped the mass card into her purse. The fact that Laredo was injecting himself into the investigation on all levels was not lost on her.

"I thought you were just investigating Eileen's murder," she reminded him.

"They all seem to be connected. I might as well try to help."

She didn't see him as the altruistic type. "I bet you were a Boy Scout when you were a kid."

It was meant as a sarcastic remark. She wasn't prepared for him to seriously answer her. "As a matter of fact, I was. My mother thought it would make me a more rounded person. She thought they had a damn fine motto: Always Be Prepared."

A man who spoke fondly of his mother couldn't be all bad—even if he did burst into bathrooms. "Sounds like a nice lady."

A quiet note of sadness fleetingly entered his eyes. "She was."

Was. As in past tense. She hadn't meant to put her foot in her mouth—or to bring up any bad memories for him. She knew what it felt like to lose a parent. The funny thing was, before he was gone, she never thought losing her father would affect her. But it had. No matter what faults he'd had, he'd still been her father.

"I'm very sorry for your loss."

Laredo had come to terms with losing his mother, but there was a measure of pain, firmly entrenched in the background. "She died a long time ago, but thanks."

Taylor found that, despite herself, she was curious about him. "Your father raise you by himself?"

He shook his head. "My father died a few years before she did. He was a Navy SEAL on a mission that didn't quite turn out the way everyone expected," he filled in before she could ask.

"Oh." He'd lost two people in his life—and she had lost her father twice. The first time around, the under-cover narcotics detective had faked his death but it had hurt just like the real thing.

"My grandfather raised me," Laredo told her, adding, "when he didn't have to."

Chester Laredo had been under no obligation to take him and his widowed mother in and definitely under no obligation to opt to raise him on his own after his mother was killed. Chet could have hidden behind the demands of his job, which were enormous, but he didn't.

"So anytime he asks me for a favor, I'm more than happy to oblige in any way I can."

Every time she tried to write this man off, he'd un-expectedly display an admirable trait. It was getting harder and harder to actively dislike him—and she felt she needed to for her own self-preservation.

Taylor nodded in response to his last comment. "Yeah, I could see why." She turned to the two patrolmen who had been first on the scene. "I'd like you to canvass the area, please," she requested. "See if anyone knew this man or saw anything suspicious." She gave each man her card. "Call me if you find out anything at all, and I mean *anything*." Done, she turned to Laredo. Funny, she thought, in an odd way she was getting used to having him at her elbow. "C'mon."

"Yes, ma'am." She couldn't make up her mind if he was having fun at her expense or not as Laredo fell into place beside her. "Mind if I ask where we're going?"

"Where we were going before I got this call," she reminded him. "To show the security guard at The Villas Terrance Crawford's picture. It's about time we caught a break."

Maybe, just maybe, the guard, Nathan, would recognize the picture and it would make him remember something that would enlighten them.

"What do you mean he's gone?"

Taylor stared at the senior security officer, Ralph Wilson, who was posted at the front desk. When she'd asked to speak to Nathan, Wilson replied that Nathan was "gone."

An uneasy feeling began to tighten in her stomach. "As in gone for the day?" she asked.

"No," the older man said in a voice that sounded raw

from forty years of smoking over a pack a day. "As in forever. The kid quit with next to no notice. Said he felt horrible about that woman being killed on his watch and that he couldn't work here anymore." It was obvious that Wilson saw what Nathan had done as being dereliction of duty, not to mention a lack of discipline and commitment. Wilson shook his head in disgust. "I tried to tell him he was overreacting, but you know these sensitive types." Wilson fairly spat out the words, leaving them hanging in the air.

There was no doubt in her mind that the man didn't think very highly of sensitivity when it came to the male gender. But she wasn't here to argue about the merits of sensitivity or its drawbacks.

"Do you have an address for Nathan?"

A spark of contempt flickered through his brown eyes. "Of course I do. We have all our employees fill out forms when we hire them."

Turning the small computer monitor on the side of the desk so that it faced him and no one else, Wilson slowly pressed several key combinations. Eventually, he pulled up the screen.

"Right here," he announced.

Taylor quickly copied down the address, aware that Laredo was looking at the screen over her shoulder.

Frowning, he addressed the security guard. "You sure this is the address he gave you?"

The guard blustered. "Of course I'm sure. All the forms are scanned into the program." Eyebrows that could definitely use a weeding narrowed, joining together over a very sharp, prominent nose. "Why?"

Laredo saw Taylor eyeing him quizzically as well. "Because, unless the city's found a new way to make buildings go up instantly, as of two weeks ago that—" he pointed to the line on the application with the street address on it "—was a warehouse. Deserted the last time I looked."

Damn it! Taylor scowled. She knew better than to doubt him now, but she still had to ask. "How do you know that?"

"Another case I was working on," he replied vaguely, adding, "nasty business." Client-investigator privilege prevented him from elaborating that he'd tracked down a fourteen-year-old kidnapping victim to the warehouse and rescued her before she could be sold into a foreign prostitution ring.

Taylor sighed. "Nathan," or whatever his name really was, had duped them. Had duped her. She hated being taken. "Are you sure?" she pressed. The sinking feeling in her stomach already gave her the answer.

Laredo glanced at the screen a second time to verify the address, then nodded. "I'm sure."

The news was not received well by the head security officer either. He strung several curses together under his breath before saying, "Why the hell would Nathan give us a false address?"

"To go along with his false name," Taylor answered, trying to bank down her frustration. Everything the so-called guard had told her was now suspect.

Why had "Nathan" lied? Unless—damn it, had she been talking to Eileen's murderer all along?

Because of the information "Nathan" had given her,

she'd wasted precious time calling florists and showing the sketch to see if anyone had noticed the phantom delivery man.

Taylor's exasperation grew exponentially. There was only one conclusion she could come to. "There was no delivery man," she said to Laredo.

He'd already thought of that, but refrained from saying it out loud since it would be like rubbing salt into her wounds.

Instead, he just nodded. "That's a distinct possibility."

Taylor swallowed a groan. Taking out her cell phone, she called the precinct, asking the operator to connect her to one of the computer technicians. Two rings later, she spoke with someone who identified himself as Larry Lopez.

"Larry, this is Detective Taylor McIntyre. I need you to get me everything and anything you can on a Nathan Miller." She paused for a second, then added, "I'm not sure if he exists."

Rather than complain or issue a disclaimer, the man on the other end sounded as if he had just become enthusiastic. "Love a challenge. Hang on, Detective, I can just put you on hold. Shouldn't take too long to find out if he exists one way or another."

Before she could tell him that she preferred being called back, Taylor found herself listening to rousing music that sounded vaguely familiar. She didn't bother trying to place it.

"Anything?" Laredo asked her when it became apparent that she was on hold.

Instead of answering, she held up her phone to his

ear. And watched him smile. She struggled to ignore how the sight stirred her on so many levels. Now was neither the time nor the place to get sidetracked. And certainly not with him. She had no doubt that the man probably thought of himself as charm personified and had a woman for every week of the calendar year.

"*The Magnificent Seven*," he said, nodding his head in approval. When she looked at him quizzically, he couldn't bring himself to believe that she wasn't familiar with it. "Great movie, remake of a Japanese classic, *Seven Samurai.*" He watched Taylor to see if any of this rang a bell for her.

It didn't.

Taylor shrugged dismissively. "I wouldn't know about that."

Laredo looked at her in disbelief. "You've never seen it?"

"That would be the implication behind *I wouldn't know,*" she agreed. The other members of her family, particularly Riley, were movie buffs. She usually watched and forgot what she viewed once the credits faded to black.

This was not something he could leave alone. "I've got it in my collection. I could screen it for you," he offered.

Oh, no, no personal time with this man. That path, she was now convinced, only led to trouble. "Maybe some other time."

"I didn't mean this minute," he told her, amusement in his eyes.

She took offense. And being on hold always made her impatient. "I don't appreciate you laughing at me, Laredo."

"I'm not laughing," he contradicted. "I'm just enjoying you."

She was spared from responding to that because at that moment, Larry came back on the line.

"I've got some good news and some bad news," the computer tech told her. "Which would you like to hear first?"

Right about now, she could definitely stand to hear some good news. The choice was not difficult. "The good news."

She tilted the cell phone so that Laredo could hear as well.

The second his head bent close to hers, Taylor felt something warm and receptive moving through her. Sharing the phone was a tactical mistake, but pulling it away would be an even bigger one.

She hoped Larry talked fast.

"Okay. The good news, Detective McIntyre, is that Nathan Miller did exist."

Taylor picked up on the only word that mattered. "Did?"

"Yes, ma'am. Nathan Miller died in 2000. He drowned while on vacation. It was a freak accident."

I just bet it was. "Terrific," she said out loud just before she flipped her phone closed.

"Think our Nathan killed the real Nathan?" Laredo asked.

It was as if the private investigator could read her mind. She definitely wasn't comfortable with that parlor trick.

"I don't know," she admitted. With a weary sigh that

came straight from her toes, she said in disgust, "Back to square one."

She expected Laredo to agree and was surprised when he said, "Not necessarily."

Chapter 10

"What do you mean, *not necessarily?*" Taylor asked.

Now that she'd agreed to let him hang around, she couldn't help wondering if he was going to make her resort to dragging information out of him. She wasn't in the mood for games.

Laredo didn't answer her.

Instead, he strode back to the security guard at the front desk. A second before he reached the man, she realized what Laredo had to be thinking.

Of course.

"The logbook," she said out loud.

Laredo glanced at her over his shoulder and grinned. "Exactly."

"Nathan" had handled the logbook, at least once in her presence when he'd picked it up to supposedly look at the previous day's sign-in sheet. That meant the man's fingerprints had to be on the book.

Along with who knew how many others, but at least it was a start.

"I'm afraid we're going to have to impound your logbook for a while," she told the retired policeman just as Laredo reached him.

Clearly on the same wavelength, Wilson nodded. "And you're going to want the fingerprints of all the other security guards so you can rule out their prints on the book."

Taylor smiled, relieved that she wouldn't have any arguments. It was nice dealing with someone who didn't immediately balk at routine police procedures. Far too many people reacted as if their personal space was being violated when asked to cooperate with an investigation.

"Yes, I am," she agreed.

Wilson took out his cell phone and pressed a button on the keypad, getting started. "I'll round them up for you."

She nodded her gratitude. "In the meantime, I'll get someone from CSI out here to collect their fingerprints." But as she took out her phone again, Laredo caught her arm, stopping her. Now what? "What do you think you're doing?"

"No need to call anyone," he told her, releasing her arm. "I've got everything we need in the trunk of my car."

We. She was getting used to that, God help her. She was also getting used to going along with him. Was that a mistake?

"The Boy Scout thing again?" she asked, flipping her

phone closed. She followed him out of the building as he went to his car.

"Absolutely."

She could hear the grin in his voice. He was probably pretty pleased with himself, but since he was being useful, she let it go.

"Your Boy Scout handbook have a theory about why there was a mass card left at the last murder and not at the other two?"

Reaching his car, he pointed his key at it and pressed the button to disarm the security system.

"Our boy is branching out?" It wasn't a statement but a question.

"Maybe," Taylor allowed. "But what does leaving the card mean?" she pressed. Not waiting for an answer, she used him as a sounding board—the way she would have used Aaron had he been there. "Mass cards are given out as keepsakes at Catholic funeral masses. The name of the deceased is printed on the front. There was no name on the card."

He had no theory, not even a good guess. "Odd sense of humor?" he suggested.

She didn't hear him. There were too many questions crowding her head. "And why St. Thomas More? Because the card was handy and he had access to it for some reason—or was there some point to it being St. Thomas rather than another saint?"

Laredo thought for a moment, sorting the vast amount of trivia he'd picked up in his lifetime. "St. Thomas was staunch about his faith. Maybe the guy that was killed strayed from the path and the killer left him

a card so that St. Thomas can show him the way back."
It was only a shot in the dark, a wild guess at best.

Taylor looked at him sharply. "So the killer was
doing a good deed?" That didn't sound likely.

Laredo opened his trunk. There were several plastic
boxes, their contents neatly organized. "Hey, even the
most rotten scum have a little bit of good in them."

Leaning against the trunk, Taylor looked in. What the
hell was this man carrying around? Frustrated in more
ways than one, she blew out a breath. "Speaking from
experience, Laredo?"

"Just the optimist in me." Finding what he needed,
he took the small box out and closed the trunk. He held
the print kit up for her benefit. "Let's get started collect-
ing prints."

Taylor fell into step beside him as they walked back
to the entrance of the building.

"I guess you are kind of a handy person to have
around." It was a compliment she paid grudgingly, but
she knew he deserved it.

Holding the door open for her, he let Taylor walk in
first. "You just beginning to notice that?"

"Don't let it go to your head," she warned, crossing
the threshold.

He followed her in. "No, ma'am."

The way he said it made her smile even though she
tried hard not to.

It wasn't lost on Laredo. He leaned his head in toward
her so that only she could hear. "See, I told you I'd
grow on you."

That was exactly what she was afraid of, she thought,

a shiver racing down her spine. And for the life of her, she wasn't able to explain, even to herself, why.

"ASAP, huh?" the crime scene investigator echoed Taylor's request back to her a little more than two hours later.

Taylor ignored the glib tone. "Sooner, if possible," she added.

The woman in the white lab coat, Wendy Allen, sighed dramatically. She waved at several neat although overwhelmingly high piles all lined up one beside the other on the steel-top table. Hardly any of the table was clearly visible.

"See all this?" she asked. "Same instructions. And they're all ahead of you." It was a blatant dismissal.

"Yes, but they're all complicated," Laredo told her, his low voice pulsing in the otherwise silent area. Taylor saw Wendy raise her eyes up to his face.

Like a flower to the sun, she couldn't help thinking. She watched as Laredo pushed the logbook toward the technician.

"This is just a matter of dusting the book for prints and comparing them to the ones Detective McIntyre's already brought you." His warm smile widened just a touch. "Should be a walk in the park for someone with your education and talents."

Taylor was about to laugh and tell him to save his breath because Wendy Allen wasn't the type of woman to have her head turned by a few flattering words. But even as she began to speak, Taylor saw the other woman, a staunch, no-nonsense technician, visibly melt. The smile on Wendy's lips was reminiscent of the girl she'd once been several long decades ago.

Wendy thought a moment, then asked, "Is this really urgent?" The question was addressed to Laredo, Taylor noted, not to her.

"Really." The single word undulated, warm and caressing, between them.

Impatience drummed through Taylor, but she held her tongue, watching.

The short-cropped hair bobbed just a little as Wendy finally nodded her head in response. "I'll see what I can do."

"That's all we can ask—" Laredo paused half a second as he read her name from the name tag on her coat "—Wendy." He underscored the name with a quick, intimate pat on her hand, and then he withdrew, the words, "Thank you," echoing in his wake.

Her breath all but gone, Taylor turned on her heel and hurried after the private investigator. He was out the door before she caught up.

"Aren't you ashamed of yourself?" she demanded once they were clear of the lab entrance and headed toward the elevator.

He slowed his pace slightly. "Why?"

He asked the question so innocently, for a second she thought he was oblivious to the effect he'd had on the crime scene investigator. But that was like the sun not knowing it cast light.

"Because—because you came on to her to get her to process my evidence first," Taylor accused him.

He still looked like the picture of innocence. "No, I

just stated your case for you." And then, because she seemed not to get it, he elaborated. "I *talked* to her as if she was a talented woman instead of a faceless technician." Reaching the elevator bank, he pressed the button on the wall. "People respond to that."

The man wasn't fooling her. He was anything but innocent here. "Don't you mean that *women* respond to that?"

He looked surprised at the attempt to differentiate. "Women are people, too." And then he smiled. "You're doing it again."

"Doing what?" Taylor demanded. She was struggling to hold her temper in check. What *was* it about this man that set her off so easily each and every time? She could be perfectly fine and halfway into a conversation with him, she started seeing red.

"Shooting sparks from your eyes." He paused to take the sight in. "You know, you're magnificent when you're angry."

Taylor rolled her eyes. She expected more from him than something so mundane. "That has got to be the most trite saying—"

The smile on his lips made the words on hers evaporate. "Doesn't make it any less true."

They stood by the elevator, but it might as well have been in the middle of a deserted island for all the foot traffic there was at the moment. For no particular reason—other than the look in his eyes—Taylor suddenly felt completely isolated.

Completely alone with a man who raised her body temperature with a single raise of his eyebrow. Completely alone and thinking of only one thing. That she wanted him to kiss her.

And then, the next second, Taylor wasn't thinking it. Wasn't thinking at all. She was too busy reacting to having her thoughts suddenly materializing and taking shape.

Laredo had cupped her face in his rough hands and had brought his mouth down to hers, even as his eyes held hers. Her lids fluttered shut at the moment of contact.

Fluttered shut just as her heart stopped beating for a long moment, then resumed with a vengeance, pounding so hard she was afraid that her heart would make a break for freedom and pop right out of her chest.

The rest of her wasn't interested in freedom. It was only interested in prolonging these wonderful sensations that she'd believed were possible only in dreams. Because this didn't exist in real life. She'd kissed enough men to know that. To know that magic and lightning and whatever else went into fictional accounts of men and women lost in the heat of a kiss didn't take place in the real world.

Every man who had ever kissed her hadn't even managed to set off a minor rumble, much less be instrumental in an earthquake that made every part of her weak as it sent her head spinning.

The earth actually moved. And then caught on fire.

Why did this man set her world on fire? Why did it have to be this particular irreverent man who caused such chaos in her world?

"Magnificent," Laredo murmured again as he finally drew back.

The elevator had arrived and its doors had opened. Having stood the obligatory several seconds, the elevator car began to close its doors again. Laredo stuck his arm in between the two steel plates that were drawing closer, interrupting the beam that governed the process. Touching his arm, the doors sprang all the way open again.

Coming to, still dazed, Taylor managed to turn on her heel. She crossed the metal threshold, walking into the elevator car. She was grateful for the several seconds of silence that ensued as she valiantly worked to pull herself together.

Had she had the strength, she would have cursed Laredo from the bottom of her soul.

This was the second time he'd kissed her and both times he had, she found herself transforming from an intelligent, highly capable, extremely logical and sharp police detective to some tongue-tied idiot who was nothing but a mass of conflicting feelings, functioning without a single coherent thought in her head.

The silence abruptly ended as they got out on the third floor.

"It can't end here, you know," Laredo told her as they started to walk to the end of the hall, where her squad room was located.

Relieved to be talking about work, she seized on the topic. "It doesn't. There's a trail out there somewhere that'll lead us to Nathan-whoever-he-really-is. The way I see it, he's the most logical candidate for the three murders." But when she spared Laredo a glance, she saw that he was shaking his head.

"I'm not talking about that," he told her quietly. "I'm talking about us."

A blast of heat passed over her, singeing her very soul.

"Us?" she echoed. Trying her best, Taylor banked down the nerves jumping around inside of her. The last thing she wanted was for them to be visible to this man who was to blame for it all. "There is no 'us,' Laredo."

"Oh, yes there is," the infuriating man contradicted. "You can tell yourself anything you like, Detective McIntyre, but there most definitely is an 'us.' Moreover, I think you know where this is going, too."

She stopped walking and glared at him. Why was he messing with her mind this way? "To hell on a toboggan?"

"Maybe eventually," Laredo allowed.

He never looked at relationships beyond a few days at a time, knowing he could count on nothing but himself. The uncertain world he'd lived in as a child had taught him that. After his mother had been killed in that automobile accident, he'd gotten up early every morning for a year and sneaked into his grandfather's bedroom. Not to crawl into the man's bed, but just to assure himself that his grandfather was still alive, still breathing. And then, reassured and relieved, just as quietly he'd tiptoe back out again.

"But before then…" Laredo's voice trailed off, allowing her to fill in the blanks.

"There is no before then, either," she told him tersely. "Look, I'm not one of those women—like Wendy, apparently—who are going to drop like some fly at your feet. For one thing, I have a mind. For another, I've got a killer to catch. Nothing else," she emphasized, "is going to get in the way of that." She took a breath. "Now, if you can help me with that, fine. If you can't,

I'll thank you to get out of my way, stop trying to distract me and let me do my work."

"Distract you?" he repeated, amused.

She threw up her hands and started walking again. Quickly. She'd said too much.

Taylor was aware that Laredo didn't drop back, didn't turn and head back toward the elevator. Instead, he quickened his gait until he caught up and was walking right next to her. Going in the same direction she was. Obviously, he'd opted to keep working with her.

She had no idea if that was a good or a bad thing. To an extent, he had destroyed her ability to think logically and coolly at all times. The man was like a burr under her saddle. And she was going to have to live with that.

For now.

Drawing a deep breath, she marched into the squad room and let the din absorb her.

One of the detectives she occasionally worked with looked up the moment she entered. Kevin Wong rose and crossed to her before she had a chance to toss her purse into her drawer.

"I was just about to call you," he told her. "You got a hit."

It took effort not to look behind her, at Laredo. God, she hoped that she didn't look as flustered as she felt.

"Come again?" she asked Wong.

In response, he dropped a folder with several pages in it on her desk. He smiled, obviously glad to be the bearer of positive news.

"Those prints on the dead homeless guy came back with a hit."

Marie Ferrarella 145

"That was fast." She picked up the folder, opening it. "Criminal record?" she asked just before she began to scan the pages herself.

After making eye contact with Laredo, Wong looked back at her and nodded. "Yeah. His name's Hank Dougherty. Or was. Been in trouble with the law ever since he stole his first car for a so-called joyride at the tender age of fourteen. He was two weeks shy of his fifteenth birthday," Wong supplied. "I was bored," he explained when she glanced at him quizzically. "It looked like interesting stuff."

"If you say so," she murmured. "And he's certainly not going to be in trouble with the law anymore."

Without bothering to sit down, Taylor scanned the next page and the few lines that were on the third before dropping the file back down on her desk.

Just another penny-ante crook, not worth anyone's second glance. Why was he singled out by the killer? Why that method, why that card?

"Okay," she said more to herself than to the detective who'd brought her the file, "I need to find out everything I can about Mr. Hank Dougherty and if there's anything at all that ties him to Eileen Stevens and/or our teacher of the year, Terrance Crawford."

At first glance, her gut feeling was that Hank Dougherty wasn't tied to the other two victims at all. The man was older, homeless, and looked as if the only contact he might have ever had with people from either Stevens's or Crawford's world would be to ask them for any spare change, but you just never knew.

"Why don't I take care of that for you?" Laredo offered, which seemed to surprise Taylor. He opened the file, spreading out the pages so that he could quickly go over each one. "I've got someone who's pretty good about filling in the blanks in people's histories. Especially if," he added, glancing at the first page of the printout, "there's a social security number to work with."

A social security number went a long way in making things easier for his contact. Or rather, his grandfather's old contact.

Old spies didn't die, Laredo thought with a smile, they just went into security work.

Taylor wanted to turn him down, wanted to send Laredo packing and on his way. But she couldn't. She needed help and she knew it. Solving the case took precedence over her pride every time. It was just a hard fact of life. But she didn't have to like it. Especially when something told her that she was allowing herself to slide into a dangerous situation without taking proper precautions.

"Thanks," she said. "But the file doesn't leave my sight," she stipulated.

He seemed all right with that. "Then neither will I," he told her, gathering the pages back together and closing the folder around them.

A catchphrase from a hokey old science fiction series that lived in perpetuity on one of the classic cable channels came echoing back to her: *Danger, Will Robinson. Danger!*

Amen to that. She was stuck with him in close proximity—and it was all her own doing.

Yet, when Laredo sat down at her missing partner's

desk and made himself comfortable as he got down to work, it somehow seemed natural to her.

She wasn't too tired to recognize that was a very dangerous sign. She was really going to have to stay on her guard from here on in.

Chapter 11

Taylor had trouble concentrating. Try as she might to shut out all outside distractions, she couldn't. Ordinarily, she was pretty good at tuning out everything else and focusing only on what demanded her attention front and center.

But this time, her power of concentration had abandoned her.

Most of the people in the squad room had gone home for the night, but Laredo, the source of her distraction, was still there, still sitting across from her. There was a decent separation between them, yet he felt closer than her own skin. At least, to her.

And if that wasn't enough, there were occasional, low-pitched sounds coming from what was really Aaron's computer. What *was* that?

Unable to stand it, Taylor pretended to go to the coffee machine just to catch a glimpse of whatever it was that was transpiring on the computer screen.

Laredo was playing solitaire.

A card game?

"You can do that at home, you know," Taylor informed him tersely, her supposed planned trip to the coffee machine all but forgotten.

"I know," he answered cheerfully, "but then I'd have to come back once I got that information you need, so I might as well just hang around and stay put. Save on gas and all that," he'd added, slanting a quick glance in her direction.

As if I'd believe that he cared about things like the price of gas, Taylor thought, annoyed. What was he, twelve? "Why don't you find something better to occupy your mind? Something intelligent?"

"I'm saving myself for the case," he told her, unfazed by the accusation in her voice. "Besides, cheating in solitaire takes a certain sharpness."

Her eyes widened. The man was unbelievable. "You're cheating?"

"Half the fun," he responded. "Otherwise, this is a deadly dull game." Pausing, he turned around in his chair to face her. "Where're you going?"

Did he think she was making a run for it? She supposed it wasn't such a bad idea, but she had visions of him coming after her, popping up in the most inappropriate places.

She fell back to her initial excuse. "To the coffee machine. I wasn't aware that I had to run that by you first."

"You don't." Leaning forward, he took his wallet out of his back pocket and opened it. Laredo removed a couple of bills and held them out to her. "And I wouldn't mind a cup myself."

Taylor's eyes narrowed. Now he thought she was his gofer? "Then, unless you have some magical ability to make containers of coffee appear when you snap your fingers, I suggest you get up and get your coffee yourself."

"No problem. Lead the way," Laredo said, rising. "It'll be on me."

Now that was a very tempting picture. After a moment, she relinquished the thought.

Taylor walked out into the hall and led the way to the vending machine.

By the end of the day, it felt as if they were all but hermetically joined at the hip. Except for an occasional break, when he paused to talk to one of the detectives— did *everyone* know this man but her?—Laredo remained at Aaron's desk, playing solitaire and occasionally sitting up straighter and hitting a couple of keys or more on the keyboard, pulling up things she couldn't see. He would make notes then and look more serious.

But he volunteered nothing and she'd be damned if she was going to come across like some needy person and ask him what he was doing. After all, it wasn't as if she didn't have anything to do on her own.

But, when six o'clock rolled around and almost everyone from the day shift had left, Taylor decided it was time to stop playing this useless charade.

Taking her purse out of the double bottom drawer,

she placed it dramatically on top of her desk and rose from her chair. "It looks like your friend isn't going to get back to you today."

Laredo raised his eyes from the screen. The next moment, they had locked with hers. "*Today* is not over yet."

Did he have to give her an argument about everything? "Maybe not, but my shift is and I'm going home." She looked at him pointedly. He made no move to get up. The man's middle name most definitely had to be Difficult, not Chester. "Look, I can't just leave you here," she told him flatly. "No matter what you think of yourself, you *are* a civilian and you can't be here without someone on the force babysitting you."

Laredo inclined his head, as if that was logical. And then he suggested, "Then stay."

The hell she would. She was drained and needed a break. All the details she'd been reviewing had begun to run together. She needed some time to let things gel.

"I stopped babysitting when I was a teenager," she informed him.

His smile moved along his lips slowly, unfurling a hint of an inch at a time. And peeling something apart inside of her as she watched.

Most of all, Taylor thought, she needed a break from him.

"You must have been something else back then," he speculated.

She could all but see him envisioning her and nearly told him to stop it. But she had no doubt that Laredo would give her some innocent response and she'd look like an idiot.

Sparing herself the grief, Taylor said, "I was a lot more patient back then. Now let's go. If you have your heart set on it, you can continue playing this game tomorrow—" she tapped the screen "—but for tonight, you—"

That was when his cell phone rang and she was forced to let the end of her statement go unsaid. A part of her suspected he'd managed to get his phone to ring on cue, but she hadn't taken her eyes off him for the last five minutes.

Another reason to get rid of him, she thought. Because the more she watched him, the more he affected her on a deep level. She was more comfortable on her own.

The look on Laredo's face as he talked to the person on the other end of the line told her it was the call he'd been waiting for.

"Great," Laredo enthused. "I knew you'd come through, Levi. E-mail all that to me. Right, I'll tell Chet you said hi. Come over sometime," he invited. "He's itching to talk about the 'good old days,' now that they're in the past," Laredo added with a short laugh. "I owe you one. Okay, two," he amended. And with that, Laredo ended the call, closing the phone and putting it back into his pocket.

It hadn't been easy, holding on to her questions. Now that he'd hung up, Taylor pounced. "Levi?"

Laredo appeared preoccupied as he nodded in her direction. "Someone my grandfather used to work with," he told her as he typed something on the keyboard.

When he said nothing further, she prompted, "You told him to send it to you. That means you have to go home to your computer—"

That was when he actually looked at her. "You're kidding, right?"

She knew damn well so-called guest accounts could be forwarded to other computers and resented his implying that she was a computer virgin. "'Hoping' is more like it," she countered.

One glance at the computer in front of Laredo showed her a screen filled with data. For now, she forgot how annoying she found him and started reading. The amount of background facts was overwhelming.

"Where did he *get* all this stuff?" she asked, stunned as the wealth of information continued to materialize. It looked as if their homeless man had been thoroughly researched from the moment of his birth to a single mom in Kansas City until he'd drawn his last breath sometime last night—if the coroner's estimation was accurate about the latter.

"If he told you, Levi'd have to kill you," Laredo deadpanned, then felt compelled to add with admiration, "The man's good."

"The man's incredible," she breathed, leaning in closer as she read. Without realizing it, she placed her hand on Laredo's shoulder.

"A lot of that going around," she heard him say in a voice that didn't match the one he'd just been using. And then it hit her like a lightning bolt: she was practically bending over him, her hair sweeping along his shoulder. Touching his face.

The second she became aware of how close she was to him, Taylor pulled her shoulders back and snapped into a rigid position—or at least that was the plan.

But for some reason, her body wasn't getting the message and it definitely wasn't cooperating. If anything, it rebelled against her.

As if paralyzed, she remained exactly where she was, her face inches from his. And now that she'd turned her head, she was even closer than a sigh.

Taylor felt his breath on her skin. Her stomach did a backward flip, then was all but lost in the ensuing tidal wave.

"Nice job," she murmured and almost became undone by the smile that began in Laredo's sky-blue eyes and then descended to his lips.

"On behalf of Levi, thank you," he said. "And, in the words of the immortal Al Jolson, 'you ain't seen nothin' yet.'"

The name meant nothing to her. She looked at him blankly. "Who?"

"You're serious?" It was only half a question. Laredo shook his head, doing his best to suppress an amused grin. "Oh, Detective McIntyre, I fear that your education has been woefully inadequate."

He had to be the one who was kidding. "Because I've never seen *The Magnificent Seven* and I don't know who Allen Jolson is?"

"Al," he corrected her. "His name was Al Jolson and he appeared in the first talking picture. His real first name was Asa—"

She held her hands up, as if to physically fend off the

avalanche of words she felt sure was forthcoming. "How do you *know* all these things?"

His eyes crinkled. So did her stomach. Since when were they connected? "I read a lot."

Obviously all the wrong things, she couldn't help thinking. "And just how full of useless trivia is your head?" she asked.

Too late she realized that she had set herself up. Sure enough, Laredo was quick to seize the opportunity. "Why don't we go someplace for a late dinner and you can find out?"

That was the last thing she wanted. Because he was growing on her. Because she didn't have the strength to hold him at bay indefinitely. Because she *knew* she didn't have the strength to hold herself in check.

"Tempting as that is," she told him glibly, "I'm just too exhausted." She pointed to the screen. "Print that up for me and we'll call it a night."

His hands moved. Laredo began the printing process without bothering to look at the keyboard, all his attention focused on her.

"You've got to eat," he pointed out. "Keep your strength up."

Taylor shrugged carelessly. "I'll pick something up on the way home."

His next words stopped her cold. "Sounds good. You talked me into it."

About to go to the printer that serviced her side of the room, Taylor turned around to glare at him. "I wasn't trying to talk you into anything," she protested.

But he winked at her, slicing through sheets of

would-be resistance. "You're more subtle than you give yourself credit for."

Rising, Laredo crossed to the printer before she could. Something else that surprised her. She fisted her hand at her waist.

"How is it that you know where the printer's located and you didn't know where the coffee machine was?" she asked. The printer wasn't out in plain sight but housed in a cubicle against the far wall. The coffee machine, on the other hand, was out in plain sight on the way to the elevators.

"Priorities?" he suggested innocently.

Taylor sighed and shook her head. Though she hated to admit it, she just wasn't up to arguing with this man. Not when she knew that she'd wind up losing. It occurred to her that, like it or not, she had finally met her match.

J. C. Laredo had the ability to effectively wear away his opponent. If she hadn't been on the receiving end of that talent, she might have even admired it. But she *was* on the receiving end and that meant only one thing. She was going to have to stay on her guard.

Constantly.

So what was she doing, letting him tag along as she went home? Somewhere along the line from the precinct to her apartment door, she'd lost her focus. And quite possibly, her mind. Otherwise, she would have sent Laredo packing long before she pulled up into her apartment complex, his vintage vehicle behind her.

Not for a minute was she buying his excuse—that he wanted to read through Levi's pages after she was finished with her initial perusal. If that was the case, they could have printed up two sets. But, if it wasn't for him, she wouldn't have had this information. At least, she wouldn't have been able to get her hands on it this quickly.

Besides, she silently argued, pulling into her parking space, she wouldn't allow herself to be distracted. And as long as they just talked about the case, what could happen?

That she'd wanted to take the night off mentally was not forgotten. The best laid plans of mice and men and homicide detectives…

The tempting aroma of still-hot Chinese food all but surrounded her as she unlocked the door to her apartment. Laredo came in right behind her. He carried an open rectangular box filled to the brim with four different cartons of Chinese food, as well as the obligatory egg rolls, egg drop soup and half a dozen fortune cookies. The last items were thanks to the cashier. The young woman had rained the individually wrapped cookies into the box after the unusually generous tip that Laredo slipped into her hand registered.

He set down the box in the center of the kitchen table.

"Damn that was hard," he said more to himself than to her.

She looked at him over her shoulder. "The box was heavy?" she asked, confused. His comment made no sense to her. While not muscle-bound, she'd noted more than once that the man had one hell of a physique.

"No, but the food was tempting as hell," he told her. He emptied the box, placing the contents around the perimeter of the table. "Took everything I had not to start sampling it in the car."

She laughed shortly. "Your restraint is admirable," Taylor quipped.

She didn't expect to get trapped in his eyes when he raised them to hers and said, "You don't know the half of it."

She made a tactical error by looking into his eyes. She had to avoid that from now on if she wanted her knees to make it through this evening. Taking a breath to hopefully clear her head, she breezed past him to the kitchen cupboards. Another fortifying breath went in, then out and she began to take down two plates and the same number of forks, spoons, napkins and glasses.

Taylor set everything she'd brought back on the table beside the cluster of cartons and announced in a voice that was just this side of hollow, "Well, you can dig in now."

"Can I, now?"

She forgot her promise to herself about not looking into his eyes.

The inside of her mouth turned to cotton but she refused to explore why. Like the man said, she needed to eat to keep her strength up. Right now, she felt as if she had the strength of a newborn kitten.

What *was* wrong with her?

Where were all these adolescent feelings and reactions coming from? She was closer to thirty than twenty, for heaven's sake, and these feelings weren't even worthy of a twenty-year-old. Not even a very *young* twenty-year-old.

"Yes, you can," she said as if he hadn't just begun to melt her inner core. "After all, you paid for it." She was doing her best to focus on the food and not on the way her pulse beat erratically. "And besides, I can't eat all this by myself." As if to tempt him—or was that distract him—Taylor pushed one of the sealed containers toward his plate. "I think that's sesame chicken."

He smiled as he opened the container. "Sesame chicken it is." He took a little onto his plate, mingling it with flavored rice. "You had a twenty-five percent chance of being right."

"Better odds than I usually have," Taylor couldn't help commenting under her breath.

"Oh?" He reached for another container at the same time she did. He withdrew, indicating that she could go first. "Is that professionally or—?"

"That's off-limits, Laredo," she informed him, shoving the second container into his hand to underscore her point. "You're here because somehow you managed to inject yourself into my investigation and I'm too polite to show you your walking papers. But if you think for one moment this gives you a free pass to do or ask anything you damn well feel like—and expect me to answer—you couldn't be more wrong."

"Finished?" he asked mildly. She looked at him quizzically. "Are you finished?" he repeated, then rephrased his question. "Did you get that out of your system? Yelling at me, I mean."

"For now. Although I reserve the right to do it again the next time you deserve it," she informed him as she took a serving of chicken lo mein. There was no question about it, the man aroused her curiosity—among other things. "Why?"

He took the lid off the container of egg drop soup and passed it to her. "Because I have a question for you."

She watched the overhead light dance along the top of the soup. The beams of light mingled with the steam. It was still too hot to eat. "Go ahead."

"Can I kiss you?"

Okay, *not* what she expected to hear. It took all she had not to let her jaw drop. Finding her voice took another good half a minute. She did her best to sound blasé. "Why are you asking? You didn't the other two times."

"Because we're on your home ground now. And because there are other factors that'll come into play this time around," he told her meaningfully. "Now, can I kiss you?" he repeated, his voice low, soft. Caressing her.

Creating incredible havoc throughout her soul.

"Go ahead," she whispered, her breath catching in her throat even before he raised her to her feet and brought her close to him.

Chapter 12

Taylor realized she was a woman standing at the very edge of a narrow ledge. Moreover, she was about to go plummeting without the benefit of even a rubber band to anchor her in place.

When Laredo's lips touched hers, she instantly felt herself free-falling into the abyss, an almost giddy sensation filling every nook and tiny crevice within her. The emptiness Taylor carried within her instantly vanished.

The kiss between them blossomed, drawing in all her senses. She could taste him, feel him, breathe in the particular scent of him. She was vaguely aware of the shampoo he used for his hair, his aftershave and soap.

The subtle mix made her head spin—or was that the effect of the kiss that was ever deepening? Or was it because of the man who was holding her to him as if there were no barriers between them?

All she knew was that they were already mingling, already becoming one even though they hadn't even gone beyond the kitchen, hadn't gone beyond the press of lips to lips.

It felt as if they were already miles beyond that.

He was making love to her with his mouth.

Taylor's pulse raced madly as she tightened her arms around his neck. She kissed Laredo back for all she was worth. There was no way she intended to be the passive one here, the only one who got her shoes knocked off. Although she secretly admitted that she didn't possess nearly the kind of experience as that of the other women he must be used to, her instincts kicked in with full force.

Laredo had known that he'd wanted her even before he'd kissed Taylor in front of the restaurant. He'd known right from the first minute he'd come upon her talking to herself in Eileen's apartment. Something about the sharp police detective with the smart mouth had pulled him in almost immediately. This was what real chemistry was all about.

He could fight it for just so long.

Out in public, he could hold that need, that desire that coursed through his veins whenever he was around Taylor, in check. Even when he was a teenager, he hadn't believed in putting on a show for others to watch, which meant that he developed iron control and never allowed himself to get carried away.

But now they were away from prying eyes.

Behind closed doors, in the privacy of her apartment,

a different set of parameters came into play and he could feel his steely control slipping away from him. It bothered him that his control wasn't relaxing any more because he could finally kiss her. Instead, it just disappeared of its own volition. As if he had no say in the matter.

While there was still a slender thread of control left, Laredo drew his lips away from hers, ignored the frantic hammering of his heart and looked down at this woman who stirred his blood.

"You're sure?" he whispered.

Because her brain was on a holiday, it took Taylor a second to make sense of the words. To focus her mind as well as her eyes.

When she did, she was still confused. Why did he feel the need to question her? Couldn't he sense her willingness?

"I didn't take you for someone so PC," she finally said.

"Not PC," Laredo contradicted. "I just don't believe in taking advantage." The ultimate pleasure came in sharing the experience, not in selfishly focusing on his own needs.

Taylor still would have never believed it if she hadn't actually witnessed it. Even so, she found herself not wanting to be a witness. For once in her life, she didn't want to have time to think, to examine the situation from every single angle. She wanted the sexy investigator to continue sweeping her off her feet.

Most of all, she didn't want to be conscious of making a decision. She just wanted the tidal wave of emotions, of feelings and desires, to carry her away. Right now, the level of passion within her was almost overwhelming.

"More Boy Scout qualities," she murmured, her mouth once more less than an inch from his.

"Hard thing to turn off." Even so, he was having one hell of a time resisting her lips. Especially since she kept grazing his with them. He could feel his pulse quickening each time she did so.

"Try," she breathed just before she kissed him with the full force of everything churning inside of her.

The next moment, she felt herself being raised up off the floor. Taylor took the opportunity to seal her body to his, wrapping her legs around his torso, her arms more firmly around his neck.

When he moved his mouth from hers and began kissing her eyelids, the hollow of her throat, the hint of cleavage that peered out above her blouse, Taylor felt her breathing become even more erratic. A moan filled with pleasure and anticipation escaped her lips.

She would have very easily testified that she was on fire.

On fire and incinerating fast.

Sliding her body back down until her feet touched the floor again, Taylor brought her mouth back up to his. As she did, her fingers worked away the clothing that kept his body from hers.

The feel of his hands on her body rendered her intoxicated with almost painful longing. She hardly recognized herself. But it didn't matter. Nothing mattered except this delicious sensation.

A long, hot shiver shimmied up and down her spine, creating goose bumps on her arms as she surrendered first her blouse, then her slacks. Hurrying to keep up, she tugged the shirt she'd opened down Laredo's arms and then worked his belt loose. All her fingers had turned into thumbs.

Something scrambled within her, rushing toward a goal she couldn't define or even put into words.

This was just about making love, right? The idea that it was more than that terrified her. But she couldn't call a stop to it, couldn't back away.

Her intake of breath was sharp as Laredo's capable, rough hands gently cupped her breasts.

When had he taken off her bra?

Taylor fought to keep up.

The feel of his chest rubbing against hers almost completely undid her, creating bolts of lightning streaking through her.

Damn, he couldn't remember the last time he'd gotten so carried away. Couldn't remember the last time he had to struggle not to go under, losing his very thought process. It wasn't that he laid out lovemaking like a military campaign, but there were definitely steps involved to please a woman, to heighten her pleasure until they finally came together as one.

Right now, the steps, the plan, eluded him. This blue-eyed wonder kept doing things to him that made his brain all fuzzy. She was a living, breathing contradiction in terms, touching him with an urgency that was still almost hesitant. Almost shy.

It was, he thought, as if he was making love with two different women. Taylor McIntyre was far more complicated than he'd initially expected.

But he wasn't complaining. Not by a long shot. He couldn't remember the last time that the very act leading up to the final experience had been so exhilarating, so exciting. He was like an adolescent again, struggling to hold back in order to appreciate the full impact.

With superhuman effort, Laredo drew his lips away from hers. "Where's your bedroom?"

Her knees sinking, Taylor realized that he was asking her a question. For the life of her, she couldn't make any sense of it. His words buzzed in her head.

"What?" she breathed.

"Bedroom," he repeated huskily. "Where is it?"

He didn't know just how much longer he could restrain himself. Although it had never bothered him before, somehow, it didn't seem right to make love with her right here in the kitchen, or even on the living room floor.

He wanted their first time to be in her bed.

That he was thinking in terms of numbers didn't register just then. If it had, he would have realized that he had good reason to be concerned. And afraid, because that was what the thought of commitment did to him.

Rather than answer—she honestly didn't think she could—Taylor pointed in the general direction of her bedroom. And then she took his face in her hands and kissed him long and hard.

Shattering his concentration. Laredo almost lost it then. Despite his latest resolve, he almost took her right then and there on the kitchen table.

Feeling weak-kneed—when had that ever happened before?—Laredo scooped this woman who unaccountably rocked his world into his arms and carried her in the direction she'd pointed.

The second they were in her bedroom, he laid her

down on the bed and then joined her, covering the soft contours of her body with the hardened ones of his. When she twisted beneath him in response, Laredo knew he had very little time left.

With all but his last ounce of strength, he drew back, creating a whisper of a space between them. His body throbbing, he swiftly and thoroughly anointed her damp body with soft, warm, openmouthed kisses along her skin.

Stifling a cry, Taylor began to twist and wiggle more urgently than before.

Something happened to her that she'd never experienced before. For lack of a better description, explosions went off inside of her, originating in her very core. Delicious, mind-melting explosions that bathed her body in heat and ever-growing desires.

Stunned as one explosion flowered into another, growing in intensity, Taylor cried out his name and then pressed her body urgently against his. More than anything, she wanted the sensation of sweet agony to go on forever, even though she knew that wasn't possible.

Her breathing close to erratic, she was only vaguely aware that Laredo had slipped his arms around her, drawing his body up to hers.

And then he entered.

And abruptly stopped.

Stunned, Laredo looked down at the woman who had thrown him for such a loop. He wasn't an expert in this department, but he knew physical resistance when he encountered it.

Pivoting on his elbows, he drew his head back even further, still looking down at her.

It wasn't possible.

Was it?

After a second he found his voice and hoarsely asked, "Are you…?"

Laredo never got a chance to finish the awkward question. Taylor knew she only had a second, maybe two before he pulled back completely. The man had already proven that he wasn't the type to force himself on a woman no matter how aroused he was. And more than anything, she didn't want him to stop.

The moment she had said "Go ahead," Taylor knew she had made the conscious decision that Laredo was the one. The one she wanted to make love with for the first time. No other man had ever gotten her to come even close to this point.

But Laredo had and there was no way she was about to allow him to retreat and abandon her. Not when they both wanted it so much.

"Stop talking," she breathed. Hardly a whisper, it was still a direct order.

Taking his face in her hands again, she brought her mouth up to his even as she began to twist her body urgently against his.

Needs and desires sprang up again, taking up the places they had just temporarily, with the greatest reluctance, abandoned.

Laredo knew the difference between right and wrong. He judged that he probably had a better sense of it than most of the people he encountered in his line of work. But he couldn't do the right thing here, the noble thing, and just walk away. Not when she'd just melted his bones, rubbing that near-perfect body of hers against his.

Biting off a curse, he pushed himself into her, holding her so close his heartbeat became hers. He began to move his hips in time with the near-frantic movement of hers.

Desires and passions grew to unmanageable proportions, absorbing him.

Absorbing her.

When the final moment arrived a handful of heartbeats later, the sensation sent Laredo spiraling off into another world where only pleasure existed. But that world began to fade even from the very moment it had materialized. The real world rose up to greet and claim him. Sadly, all but blotting out the other.

Euphoria receded even though, now more than ever, he wanted it to linger.

As it faded, it ushered in a sense of guilt in its place. A guilt that was so tangible, he could almost touch it.

Falling back, he remained next to her. Searching for words that could somehow make this up to her. None occurred to him.

"I'm sorry," he finally said, his tone all but stilted.

Taylor immediately propped herself up on her elbow and looked at him. So many emotions swirled through her, it almost made her dizzy. She struggled to brace herself for what she knew was coming, but even as she tried, she knew she was woefully unprepared for the way it would hurt.

"You're 'sorry,'" she echoed. "Sorry for making love with me?" she asked.

The last thing he'd wanted to do was to bring her pain—

emotionally *or* physically. "Why didn't you tell me?" When she didn't answer, Laredo repeated the question. "Why didn't you tell me that you were a virgin?"

Right. As if that was the kind of thing you talked about. Why was he putting her through this? Why couldn't he just pretend he'd enjoyed himself?

"The opportunity never worked itself into the conversation," she bit off.

Oh, but it had, he thought. "Just now, in the kitchen, when I asked if I could kiss you, you couldn't tell me then?"

Okay, now she was angry. Anger had come to her rescue, springing out of embarrassment to shield her. "You mean why didn't I say, 'Yes you can kiss me if you want to but you might not want to because I'm a virgin and I'll only disappoint you?'" she asked sarcastically. "Sorry, guess I just wasn't thinking clearly at the moment."

Sitting up, Laredo stared at her as if she were suddenly speaking in some foreign language. "What the hell are you talking about?" he finally demanded. "You think I'm disappointed?"

"Well, aren't you?" she challenged.

"Hell, no."

"Then why are you yelling at me?" she demanded, yelling back. Incensed, she couldn't help herself.

"Because you should have told me." He shouldn't have to explain it to her. As a woman, she should have understood that to begin with. "There's a lot of responsibility, being a woman's first lover."

Was that it? He wasn't disappointed, he was afraid

she was disappointed in him? She would have laughed if she hadn't thought that it might have hurt his feelings. Instead, she fell back on being flippant.

"Don't worry, I won't bill you. On the upside, I have nothing to compare this to." For the first time, she grinned at him. "Which makes you the greatest lover I've ever had."

Now that the euphoria and frenzy had died back, she felt awkward. Nothing a little clothing couldn't fix, she told herself. Turning away from him, Taylor began to get up.

Laredo caught her wrist, holding her in place. His frustration over the fact that he should have gone slower, been more tender toward her, began to abate. "There is that, I suppose."

She looked down at his fingers locked around her wrist. "I can't get dressed if you're holding my wrist." She raised her eyes to his expectantly.

But he didn't release her. "I know."

She took in a breath, then let it out slowly. Some of her embarrassment began to recede, nudged away by another round of anticipation. Was this how it was? Up and down until she felt dizzy?

She looked down at his hand again. "So what is it that you have in mind?"

Taylor heard the grin in his voice. "To give you something to compare your first time to."

"Are you going to yell at me at the end of that, too?" she deadpanned.

"I wasn't yelling at you," he told her. "I was yelling at me."

Funny, it certainly felt like he was yelling at her. But now that she knew why, she wasn't upset any longer. "And what, I just got in the way?"

He lifted his shoulder in a dismissive, half shrug. "Something like that."

Removing his hand from her wrist, he reached up and gently feathered his fingers through her hair. Something stirred within him.

He wanted her again.

"A woman's first time is supposed to be special," he told Taylor. "At the very least, the earth is supposed to move for her."

Taylor pressed her lips together, debating whether or not she should be honest with him or just keep him guessing. But she had always been truthful and games were for people who were careless about other people's feelings.

"So far, so good," she finally said softly.

In response, he grinned. Laredo's smile was so sexy, she could hardly stand it. Feelings began to rush forward again, faster than the first time.

"I don't want to be good," he told her, his voice low. "Do you?"

"Good is in the eyes of the beholder," she managed.

"That's beauty," Laredo corrected, drawing her closer to him as he laid down again. "Beauty is in the eye of the beholder."

The phone could ring at any minute, calling her back to duty. Or he would suddenly realize that he had somewhere else to be. Taylor didn't want to waste precious time discussing a poem she'd long since forgotten.

"Shut up, Laredo," she murmured raising her mouth up to his.

"Yes ma'am," Laredo replied obediently.

And then the next moment, he began to devote himself to showing Taylor the right way to make love to a woman the first time around.

Slowly.

Chapter 13

Laredo considered himself a light sleeper, rendered that way both by nature and out of necessity because of the demands of his vocation. He would have thought, then, that the slightest shift of weight on the surface of the mattress, especially if someone was slipping away, would have woken him up.

But when he did open his eyes to greet the dawn, he found himself alone in the bed. Taylor was gone. From the bed and, apparently, from the room.

Surprised and a little uncertain—just because he'd made love with the woman a record number of three times, as he recalled—didn't mean that she was now an open book to him. With Taylor, he was still feeling his way around.

Right now, he wouldn't have put it past the crafty Detective McIntyre to try to get a jump ahead of him on this case by sneaking out and leaving him here, asleep at the wheel.

Laredo shook his head. He liked his women simpler, he thought as he hurried into the clothes that, unaccountably, were now sitting on a chair in the bedroom instead of scattered throughout the kitchen the way he remembered leaving them. He liked his women more predictable at least, he silently added.

Oh, yeah? I didn't see anyone holding a gun to your head to stay last night. Or urging you to go for a record-breaking performance test, either. That was all on you and you were free to leave anytime.

Zipping up his pants, Laredo sighed. Okay, so there was something about the feisty homicide detective that attracted him more than he was comfortable with. But that would pass soon, he promised himself. And then maybe things could get back to normal again.

There was no denying that he liked his life just the way it was, uncomplicated except when it came to his cases. He was committed to his work and his grandfather. That was where it ended.

As he quickly walked toward the front of the apartment, it occurred to Laredo that he was protesting a bit too strongly.

Never a good sign.

He passed the other, smaller bedroom, came to a screeching halt and then retraced his last two steps. He looked in. His eyes hadn't been playing tricks on him. Taylor was there, wearing something baggy and misshapen—an oversize police T-shirt?—sitting at a desk in front of a computer. All her attention appeared to be focused on the monitor as she scrolled down.

He wondered what had captured her attention so exclusively—but he didn't wonder that nearly half as much as he wondered if she'd bothered to put anything on underneath her T-shirt.

Visions of their lovemaking played vividly across his mind. Whetting his appetite.

Laredo entered the room and, coming up behind her, embraced Taylor lightly with one arm.

Startled, Taylor gasped and swung around.

Seeing that it was Laredo, she relaxed and said, "You shouldn't sneak up behind me like that."

He smiled. "Next time, I'll yell before I walk in." He looked at the screen that had held her attention so intently. "Anything interesting?" he asked, noting a site devoted to the Middle Ages.

"Maybe." Turning her chair around to face him, Taylor leaned back and said, "Did you know that, among other things, St. Thomas More is the patron saint of adopted children?"

She'd lost him. Laredo looked at her quizzically, then remembered the mass card that had been found beside the last body.

"As a matter of fact, no, I didn't. Must have escaped my required reading list." He looked at the screen again, then shook his head. No bells were ringing for him. "Is that supposed to mean something to us?" he finally asked.

She wished she could say yes, but the hard truth of the matter was that she was still trying to connect the dots. "I don't know yet. I just think it's a little odd, given that the first two victims were connected because Stevens was pregnant with Crawford's baby."

He tried to connect that to the third victim. "So you think, what? That our homeless guy got Stevens pregnant, too?"

"No, but our homeless guy did get someone pregnant." It was a thin, almost nonexistent thread, but so far, the only thread they had.

Laredo looked at her. All that from a mass card? He had to be missing something. "Come again?"

Taylor began to shuffle through the array of papers all spread out on the desk beside the computer. "It's right here, in the pages that your friend e-mailed you," she told him, excitement growing in her voice. Finding what she was looking for, she began to read, "It says here that Linda Lawson accused Dougherty of being the father of her baby and tried to take him to court to collect child support. They couldn't find him. Shortly thereafter, Lawson gave the baby, a two-month-old girl, up for adoption." Taking a breath, she looked up at him. "Think it means anything?"

So far, it was just a coincidence, albeit an uncanny one. "Other than, what, there's some superhero out there avenging unwanted kids who were given away by their biological parents?"

Taylor bristled. He was laughing at her. "Not a superhero," she retorted, "but, well—have you got a better idea?"

The corners of Laredo's mouth curved. "That depends."

The way he watched her told Taylor that he might not be talking about the same thing. "On what?" she asked gamely.

His smile grew, slipping into his eyes as they drifted down the length of her. Funny how he hadn't realized sooner just how long her legs really were. "On whether or not you're wearing anything under that baggy T-shirt of yours."

Taylor valiantly ignored the hot shivers suddenly racing up and down her spine. "I'm serious," she told him.

"So am I." And then he sighed, relenting. For the moment. "But maybe your idea isn't that off the wall— insofar as orphaned kids being a connecting factor. It wouldn't hurt to have a few words with the kid that Stevens and Crawford gave up for adoption—if we can track him down," he qualified.

They both knew it was a huge *if.* More and more adoptees were avidly tracking down their birth parents these days in an effort to connect with their roots. But that sort of thing usually took months if not years of diligent work and digging.

Taylor had this uneasy feeling that they didn't have months, that if she was right, another victim was going to surface soon. Most likely, that victim would be Linda Lawson.

Taylor hit a few keys and closed down her computer. "Why don't I get you breakfast," she suggested, "and then we'll see if we can locate this Linda Lawson?" She turned her chair around to face him again. "She might be able to direct us to the agency that took in her baby." Taylor shrugged, anticipating that he would call it a waste of time. "It's a start. Maybe."

About to get up, Taylor found that her limbs were frozen in place. Laredo had begun to slowly run his hand up along her leg, starting at her knee. He was at her thigh now.

Her body tingled in response. "What are you doing?" she breathed.

His smile began to unravel her. Again. "You offered me breakfast," he replied.

"Yes." She had to push the word out as it had gotten stuck in her throat.

"This is what I want for breakfast." "This" being her, she assumed.

Before she could protest, or tell him that he was going to need something more substantial to see him through the day, Laredo swept her up to her feet and against him in one smooth motion.

"Any objections?" he asked.

Because he'd asked rather than taken, he'd melted her resolve and any protest she might have had.

"No."

It was the last word Taylor uttered for quite some time.

A quick search through DMV records told them that Linda Lawson was now Linda Morrow, living not that far away from where she had originally grown up. They lost no time in getting to her.

Linda Morrow answered the door after Taylor had rung the bell twice. The onetime captain of the cheer-leading squad looked as if she had found life after high school hard and unforgiving.

She reminded Taylor of a flower that had bloomed for too long and was now beginning to wilt.

"We have a few questions we'd like to ask you,"

Taylor told her after introducing herself and Laredo. The woman seemed unwilling to step aside and allow them in. "It won't take long," Taylor pressed.

Instead of inviting them in, Linda slipped out onto the porch, closing the door behind her in the furtive manner of a woman attempting to keep her home separate from what had been dropped on her doorstep.

Linda ran her tongue nervously over her lips. "My husband's home today. Sick," she explained. "I can't talk to you," she added in a lowered, pleading voice.

Taylor took a guess. "Your husband doesn't know, does he?"

"Know? Know what?"

"That you gave a baby girl up for adoption," Laredo answered.

The thin, mousy-looking woman's eyes widened, surprised by the question. And then she shook her head. "No, he doesn't know," she said in a flat voice. "And I want to keep it that way. He's a very jealous man. I don't want to set him off."

Because of her father, Taylor immediately jumped to a conclusion. "Is he abusive?"

Again, Linda licked her lips, shaking her head. "No, no, but he's hell to live with when he gets in one of his moods." She glanced over her shoulder toward the door, as if she expected her husband to drag her inside at any second. "Please, just go away."

Taylor didn't want to put the woman in any danger, but then again, if she saw any sort of abusive behavior—whatever Linda wanted to call it—she could arrest the woman's husband.

"We'll leave just as soon as you tell us which agency you gave your baby to."

Linda shook her head. It was obvious that she couldn't remember the exact name. "I gave the baby to a social worker. I don't remember her name." Nervously, she shrugged. "She was with some government agency."

"You mean Social Services?" Laredo asked, peering at the woman's face for recognition.

Linda Morrow had the desperate manner of a woman who would grasp at anything. "Yes, that was it. Social Services. Now please, you have to go," Linda begged. Nervously, she looked over her shoulder toward the closed door again. Fear radiated from every pore.

This just wasn't right, Taylor thought. She was dying to put this woman's husband in his place. No one should have this kind of power over another human being, to make them so afraid.

"Just one more question," she pressed. "Have you seen Hank Dougherty recently?"

At the mention of the name, Linda paled visibly. "No, not since I gave up the baby. Now I really have to get back." Not waiting for a response, the woman quickly darted back into the house, firmly closing the door behind her.

Laredo made no move to leave. "You believe her?" he asked, looking at the closed door.

Taylor shrugged, turning from the door. "For now, we have no other choice." She gazed up at him, curious. "Why? Don't you?"

"I don't know yet," Laredo said honestly. "She seemed awfully jumpy to me."

Taylor laughed shortly. There was no humor in the sound. "Marriage to an abusive husband'll do that to you every time."

Laredo turned away from the house. They began to walk back to the curb where Taylor had parked her vehicle. "She said he wasn't."

"Abused women lie, Laredo. All the time. They don't want the world to know just how bad things really are. A lot of them think that it's all their fault. That if they were perfect, their husbands would have no reason to be 'displeased' with them."

Laredo stopped walking and looked at her for a long moment. He felt a wave of anger rising. Anger not directed at her but at whoever had shown her this ugly side of life.

"Is that just theory, Detective?"

She shook her head. He'd misunderstood. "I haven't been in an abusive relationship, if that's what you're asking. I would never let anyone get close enough for that to happen," she added firmly. "Doesn't mean I haven't seen one, up close and personal."

He wondered if he was included in that emotional embargo and was now on notice. She was suddenly challenging him. More questions occurred to him. He wanted to dig deeper in this stretch of soil she'd just exposed to him.

But for now, he kept his questions to himself. He'd already learned that Taylor was the type who immediately circled the wagons if she perceived an attack coming. Better to just wait and let her volunteer the information on her own. In the meantime, they had a crime to solve.

"You know," he told her, looking back at the house, "you could call that probable cause—thinking she was in some kind of danger because her husband was home." He, of course, needed no such excuse.

She followed his thinking to its logical conclusion. "And just come in like gangbusters, breaking down the front door?"

Laredo shrugged. "Sounds good to me," he said affably.

Maybe he could do it, but she couldn't. "You're a P.I., Laredo. Everything I do has to be by the book."

His smile was wicked. "Everything?"

But just then they heard a woman's scream coming from the house. The moment vanished. He looked at Taylor expectantly. "You were saying?"

"The hell with the book," Taylor retorted, pulling out her handgun and releasing the safety.

He grinned, taking out his own weapon. "Now you're talking."

Measuring the necessary space with his eyes, Laredo took a step back and then kicked in the door, hard. The lock splintered and the door hung drunkenly from the frame with only one hinge holding it up.

Taylor rushed in half a step ahead of him, her adrenaline surging. Laredo, she noted, had his gun drawn, too. She hoped he knew how to hit what he aimed for.

Nothing but eerie silence met them as they swept first one room, then another.

"Linda?" Taylor called out. "Linda, can you hear me? This is Detective McIntyre. We heard you scream and we're here to help you." Still nothing. She exchanged looks with Laredo. He nodded toward the back of the house. She raised her voice even higher. "Where are you?"

No one answered.

Something was very, very wrong. Taylor could feel all her senses going on high alert. Cautiously, they moved from one room to the next. Encountering no one.

"Linda, if you can hear me, say something," Taylor coaxed. "If your husband has hurt you in any way, you can have him arrested. We can keep you safe. He'll never get to you again. You have my word."

There was still no indication that anyone was in the house. They were almost out of rooms. Only one more left in the single-story house. The door to that room, a second bedroom, was closed.

Linda and whoever had made her scream had to be in there.

Taylor exchanged glances with Laredo, indicating that she intended on going into the room first. In response, Laredo nodded. But as she reached for the doorknob to slowly test it, Laredo suddenly rammed his shoulder against the door, causing it to fly open.

Rushing in, Laredo trained his weapon on the center of the room. Just above Linda's head.

The woman was on her knees in the middle of the room. She trembled and sheer terror shone in her eyes. A fresh strip of duct tape stretched across her mouth, sealing in her screams and turning them into whimpers.

Another woman, younger than all of them, stood behind her. Tall, thin, with mousy brown hair that hung limply on either side of her gaunt face, there appeared to be nothing remarkable about her.

Except for the gun she held in one hand and the strip of wet leather she was holding in the other. A drop of water slid down the length of the strip and dripped onto the carpet.

In its own way, the look in the younger woman's eyes was just as terrified as Linda's.

She waved her weapon at the two of them. "Get the hell out of here!" she demanded, her voice cracking at the end of her order.

Laredo's eyes never left the young woman's. "I don't think so." He took a step forward.

"Stay back," she threatened, raising her gun so that it pointed at his chest. Her hand was shaking. "I mean it! This doesn't involve you."

"Oh, but it does," Taylor told her, her voice low, almost soothing. Following Laredo's lead, she took a step toward the young woman as well. "I took an oath that said I couldn't just stand by and watch someone get killed."

"Then turn around and don't watch," the young woman snarled.

"Sorry, can't do that, either. Look—" It occurred to Taylor that she didn't even know the young woman's name. But she thought she had a pretty good idea who the woman was. "What is your name, anyway?"

Suspicion and hatred entered the dark brown eyes. "Why? You want to be my best friend?" she asked nastily.

"Not particularly," Taylor admitted. "But I need a name. Otherwise, I'm going to have to start referring to you as 'hey you.'"

The bony shoulders beneath the shabby yellow sweater rose and fell in a careless, dismissive shrug.

"Why not? I've been called worse," the young woman retorted. And then her eyes narrowed as she looked down at the woman she held at gunpoint. "And it's all this bitch's fault. Every damn bit of it."

Clearly frightened, Linda began to babble as a sob tore from her throat.

"Now is that any way to talk about your mother?" Laredo asked, shaking his head in exaggerated disapproval.

The brown eyes immediately darted in his direction. "How do you know that?" the young woman demanded. "Why did you just call her my mother?"

"Well, isn't she?" Laredo asked. "I saw it right away. The same eyes. The same hair. The same penchant for making mistakes, except that yours carry much bigger consequences for what you're about to do. This is a big mistake," he told her.

"What's a bigger mistake than throwing away your baby like it was yesterday's trash? No, worse than trash," she amended.

"She didn't throw you away," Taylor was quick to point out. "She gave you up so that you could have a better life than what she could give you. It was a huge sacrifice for her to give you up."

The hatred in the young woman's eyes as she looked down at the back of Linda's head deepened. "You believe that crap?" she demanded.

"It's not crap," Taylor countered, as calm as Linda was agitated.

The young woman's head jerked up. "Yes, it is. You want to know how much 'better' my life was because of this bitch's 'sacrifice'? I got to be passed around from one foster home to another. Treated like a servant instead of a kid. Or more like a slave," she corrected, "because at least servants are paid."

Her breathing became audible as she relived the experience. "But that wasn't the worst of it. When I was thirteen, I was sent to the Dobers. Mrs. Dober was an airhead, but she was okay. She even tried to be nice. When she wasn't drunk." Angry tears gathered in her eyes. "Her husband told me it was his job to educate me about the 'pleasures' of life. Every night, after his wife took her sleeping pills, he'd come into my room to give me another 'lesson.' I ran away four times," she said bitterly, "but every time, they'd bring me back." There was agony in her eyes. "And it just got worse."

"Why didn't you tell someone?" Laredo asked gently.

"I did," she shouted. "Nobody would believe me. Dober was a judge. His big thing was family values." The torment melted from her face as her expression darkened. "After I kill this bitch, he's next on my list."

Chapter 14

Clearly terrified, Linda Morrow began to whimper. Her trembling became almost violent, as if she were undergoing a seizure. Huge, frightened brown eyes shifted from Laredo to Taylor and then back again, like dark marbles that couldn't come to rest. They fairly pleaded for help.

"Shut up," the young woman snapped when Linda continued to whimper. She raised the wet strip, holding it in front of Linda like an unfulfilled promise. "It's time for you to pay for what you did."

Trying to divert her attention from Linda, Taylor asked the young woman, "Did you kill that homeless man they found in the alley yesterday?"

Dark, malevolent eyes shifted toward Taylor. "You mean 'Daddy'?" The woman's mouth twisted in a sardonic smile. "Yeah, I did." She paused, as if reliving the experience. "I probably did him a favor, really. The miserable drunk was so out of it, I don't even think he knew what was happening."

Realizing that Taylor was stalling, Laredo followed her lead. "Why did you kill those other two people?" he asked the woman.

The woman scowled. "What other two people?"

"Eileen Stevens and Terrance Crawford," Taylor answered. As she talked, she took in the room, trying to decide their next move. If she and Laredo separated and made their way toward the younger woman slowly enough for her not to notice, one of them might be able to catch her off guard.

The names Taylor said appeared to mean nothing to the young woman. Impatience echoed in her voice. "Who the hell is that?"

Laredo noted that Taylor had managed to move forward. He did the same, then called the young woman's attention to him, allowing Taylor to take another step forward.

"The woman in the penthouse and the teacher," he told her.

The description brought enlightenment. "Oh, them." She laughed shortly, shrugging dismissively. "I didn't kill them."

Laredo's turn to move, Taylor thought. "Same method was used," she said.

The agitated woman seemed close to the breaking point. Any opposition instantly had her temper flaring. "I said I didn't kill them," she snarled, waving the muzzle of her weapon at Taylor.

Linda was on the verge of hyperventilating. And there was no gauging what her daughter was really capable of. She looked as if she was coming apart at the seams, as unstable as a vial of nitroglycerin, Taylor thought. They needed to wrap this up somehow.

"Then who did?" Taylor probed. Out of the corner of her eye, she saw Laredo inching forward. This pace was much too slow. They needed to rush Linda's daughter. But how to keep her from firing wildly? That was the problem before them.

Linda's daughter tossed her head. "Someone who had the right to kill them," she said self-righteously.

She was talking about Eileen's son. Waiting for Laredo to say something so that she could move, Taylor glanced in his direction. He was thinking the same thing she was.

"You mean their son?" Laredo asked.

"Son," the woman snorted contemptuously. "You damn cops make it sound like some kind of PG family movie. Miles wasn't their son," she spat out the last word. "They thought he was just some mistake they made. Some*thing* they were willing to throw away."

"Miles, is that his name?" Taylor asked. She could see that the young woman was working herself up. Desperate, Taylor tried to stop the eruption she could see forming. "That's not true, you know." Taylor kept her voice low, soothing, as if she were trying to gentle a wild animal that had been hurt. And as she spoke, ever so slowly, she moved forward. "Terrance Crawford's girlfriend told us that he tried to get custody of his son, but he was too young and Eileen insisted on giving the baby up. Terrance became a teacher and devoted himself to kids in an effort to try to make up for that. Because he felt so terrible about losing his son," she emphasized.

She saw the young woman's eyes widen as she looked at something that was just behind them. Still on her knees, Linda made a gurgling noise beneath the duct tape.

"Well, well, well, let's bring out the violins," a sarcastic voice behind them said, ending the sentence with a nasty laugh. Taylor froze, as did, she noted out of the corner of her eye, Laredo.

The voice, she thought, sounded familiar.

And then she saw why. The man who'd entered the house was the missing security guard from Eileen Stevens's building.

"Nathan," Taylor cried in recognition.

"Miles," Linda's daughter exclaimed at the same time, lighting up like the proverbial Christmas tree at the very sight of him.

Joining the disheveled young woman, Nathan/Miles slipped his arm around her. In his free hand, he held a gun and aimed it at them.

There was no tremor to his hand. And his gaze was dark, flat. They were in the presence of a stone-cold killer, Taylor thought.

He brushed a kiss against his girlfriend's hair, but his eyes never left the two people still holding their weapons trained on her. "I came to see how you were doing, baby. Didn't think you were going to hold an open house."

"I'm not. I didn't," the young woman protested, irritation and nerves infusing themselves into her voice. "They just came storming in. I don't know where they came from or who they are."

"Then let me introduce you," Miles said magnanimously. "The one with the cute butt is Detective McIntyre. The guy with the scowl's some private eye. Laredo, I think his name is. Don't worry," he reassured his girlfriend, "they're clueless. They came nosing around after I offed dear old Mom."

His easy tone vanished as he raised his weapon, aiming it first at Laredo, then at Taylor. There was no doubt in Taylor's mind that he could shoot them both without the slightest qualm.

"Put your guns down," Miles barked.

"Sorry, that's not an option," Laredo told Miles before she had a chance to. Taylor held her breath. "Right now, we have a Mexican standoff. If we lower our weapons, you just pick us off one by one," Laredo pointed out, his voice deceptively calm.

Miles appeared to think Laredo's words over. "Interesting theory. You mean like this?"

And before anyone could make a move, he fired a bullet into the trembling housewife's leg. Her mouth still taped over, Linda screamed, the sound coming through her nose as she crumbled to the floor. Taylor tried to go to her, but Miles shifted the muzzle of his gun, aiming it at her. Laredo caught her by the arm and pulled her back.

"Miles!" his girlfriend cried in angry protest.

Miles laughed. "Don't worry, baby, I didn't kill her. I wouldn't rob you of the pleasure. You still get to watch her choke to death. I'm just showing these two big, bad detectives that all the cards on the table are mine. Ours," he amended as an afterthought, sparing her a nod.

Slipping his hand all the way around her, Miles deftly

extracted the gun she was holding. With a satisfied smirk, he drew back and aimed one weapon at each of them.

His eyes shifted toward Taylor. "Now put your guns down or the next shot is the kill shot."

His meaning was clear. He meant to kill Linda *and* her daughter.

Very slowly, Taylor put her weapon down before her. After a beat, Laredo unwillingly followed suit.

Triumphant, Miles nodded his head. "Now we can talk. What are our options?" he mocked. "I either snuff out your eager beaver, overachieving, worthless lives, or you end mine." He shrugged carelessly, nodding toward Linda's daughter. "And maybe Donna's."

"It doesn't have to be that way," Taylor cut in, desperately trying to reason with one of them. "We can get you help."

"Get us help?" Miles mocked. His laugh turned ugly. "Lady, are you for real? Where the hell were you when Donna was raped? Growing up in a nice little cushy home where Mama and Daddy saw to your every need?" His tone became menacing. "Where were you when I was being shoved into a wooden box in this maniac's backyard and left there, in the hot sun, for two days because I dragged a chair across the kitchen floor and left scuff marks?"

He all but got into her face, shouting, "Where were you when that son of a bitch the system gave me to beat me just 'to show me who's boss'?"

"I'm sorry that happened to you, to both of you," Taylor began. "If the system is at fault, that should be brought to the public's attention—"

"The 'public' knows. The 'public' doesn't care," Miles shouted. "They just look the other way. Your kind is responsible for everything that happened to me. To Donna. To countless other poor, dumb slobs whose only crime was to be born when they weren't wanted."

"Let the women go, Miles," Laredo requested in a mild, reasonable voice, knowing that to insist would only set the other man off. "I'll stay, I'll be your hostage. You'll need a hostage to get out of here. The police are already on their way."

"If they're as good as you two, Donna and I will be safe," he mocked. "But first—" he glanced toward the sobbing woman on the floor "—we have a little unfinished business to attend to. I went through a lot of work, finding Donna's 'birth parents.' We're not about to just walk away and let her live." Linda's sobs became louder. "Shut up, bitch!" he ordered.

"Can't you see she's sorry?" Taylor asked, taking a step forward.

Miles instantly raised the gun in his right hand. "Sorry? I'll bet she's sorry." Miles sneered at the fallen woman. "But not half as sorry as 'Mama's' going to be, I can promise you that."

"Killing her won't change anything," Taylor insisted. There had to be a way to stop this madman. She had to reason with him.

"Nope, not a thing," Miles agreed. "But it'll make Donna feel better." He spared his girlfriend a smile. "Just like killing those two rutting pigs who were my parents made me feel better."

"Did it?" Taylor challenged.

Miles scowled darkly at her. "Shut your girlfriend up," he ordered Laredo. "Or she's going to be the first to go."

Taylor opened her mouth to say that she wasn't Laredo's girlfriend, but didn't get the chance. Laredo spoke first.

"She's a police detective," Laredo reminded him. "You kill a cop, there's no place in the country that you can hide."

Miles's laugh sent a chill down Taylor's spine. "You've been watching too many cop shows on TV. That's just a lot of hype. The truth is, killers still get away with it all the time. Even cop killers." His dark eyes slanted a glance at Taylor. "They just have to be smart, that's all. And I'm smart," he bragged.

And then his satisfied smile vanished as he glanced toward Donna. "Well, what are you waiting for, Christmas? Tie that leather strip around her throat before it dries out."

Weak, frightened and losing blood, Linda still had the strength to plead for her life. She ripped the duct tape off her mouth, crying out as she did so.

"No. No, please," she cried frantically, putting both hands around her throat to keep Donna from tying the leather strip around it. "I didn't want to give you up, I didn't. You've got to believe me. I couldn't afford to keep you. I had no money, no one to turn to. You were sick. The social worker said they'd take care of you, see that you got treatment."

"Don't listen to her, baby. She'll say anything to save her life. Get this over with. We've got to go," Miles ordered.

"Don't do it, Donna," Taylor implored. Miles cocked

the gun he was aiming at her. Her hands still raised, Taylor ignored him. "Don't let him talk you into doing something you don't want to do."

Her words only incited Miles. "Who the hell are you to tell her what she wants or doesn't want to do?" he demanded.

"I'm the person who's going to go to court to testify that she was under severe duress when she killed Hank Dougherty and didn't know what she was doing." Taylor prayed that she was getting through to the other woman. Donna was clearly a weak person who could be manipulated by someone stronger willed. "They'll send you to a hospital, Donna, where you can get well. If you kill your mother, I can't help you."

"No, no more hospitals," Miles cut in. "No more institutions for us. We're finishing what we set out to do and then we're going away." He cocked his other weapon. "And you two are going to sit here and rot right along with the Mother of the Year."

Laredo knew that it was now or never. That the man on the other side of the revolvers was someone who felt he had nothing to lose. He could see it in Miles's eyes. They were flat, expressionless, as if his soul had long since vacated the premises. He was familiar with the type. Men who did desperate things because they felt they risked nothing. In their eyes, they stood to gain everything.

If he waited one more second, the results, Laredo knew, would be fatal.

With one quick motion, he pulled Taylor by the arm, pushing her behind him even as he tackled Miles. Caught off guard, the latter cursed. At the same time

Donna, afraid, screamed. One of the guns that Miles held flew out of his hand, but he discharged the other, firing wildly as he went down, backward on the floor.

Hitting his head, Miles became enraged. He scrambled up and, with a bloodcurdling shriek, lunged at Laredo. The two were approximately the same size, but Miles had learned every single dirty move in order to survive. Thin and wiry, every ounce of him was dedicated to killing.

A spectrum of colors shifted before her eyes as Taylor struggled to hold on to consciousness. The bullet from Miles's gun hadn't been fired at a target, but it had found one.

Blood was oozing out of her side, taking all her available strength with it.

She didn't have time for this, she thought, desperately trying to steel herself. *If you don't think about it, it didn't happen.*

Grabbing her gun from the floor, Taylor pointed the weapon at Donna. The latter had dropped the leather strip she'd been holding and had picked up the gun that Miles had dropped. Holding it in both hands, she aimed it at the whimpering, pleading woman on the floor.

"Drop the gun," Taylor ordered, her voice echoing in her head.

Donna looked as if she had lost the ability to process what was being said. Instead, she continued pointing her weapon at Linda Morrow. Taylor knew Donna was going to shoot her mother. Miles had told her to do it and it wasn't in the woman to disobey.

God forgive me, Taylor thought. The next moment,

she fired dead center at Donna before she could even think her action through.

Donna went down, her scream dying in her throat as she sank to her knees then fell over, her weapon slipping from her fingers. Inches separated her from her birth mother, who seemed to shrink into herself, sobbing hysterically.

Taylor turned around, trying to orient herself to what was going on behind her. The two men were still locked in combat. The pseudo-security guard had his weapon grasped in one hand. Did Laredo have his gun? She didn't see it.

Quickly scanning the floor, she noticed Laredo's weapon was still on the floor. She didn't remember racing to it, was only aware that when she bent over to pick it up, the entire room tilted dangerously, making her nauseous. She almost fell.

Hang on, Taylor, hang on. You can't pass out now, she upbraided herself sternly. *He needs you.*

Turning back again, she had to blink twice to focus on the struggling men on the floor. She had no opportunity to give Laredo his weapon.

"Back off, Miles," she ordered in what she hoped was a strong voice. "I said, back off! It's time to throw in the towel. Donna's dead. You don't want to join her. Give up. It's all over."

An unearthly, guttural wail escaped Miles's lips as, on his knees, he turned to confirm what she'd just told him. It was all the diversion Laredo needed to get the upper hand. He hit Miles hard, knocking the weapon away. Taylor hurried over and gave him his gun.

Reunited with his own weapon, Laredo motioned for Miles to get up.

Neither he nor Taylor were prepared for what happened next. Lunging forward, Miles grabbed his hand and pushed the finger that was on the trigger back.

Laredo's weapon discharged, hitting Miles point-blank in the chest.

A maniacal smile of deep satisfaction curved the man's lips as he sank back to the floor.

"Looks like I won't be going to any more institutions," were the last words Miles uttered. He fell over, lifeless.

Shaken, Laredo turned to the cowering woman on the floor.

"You're safe now," he told Linda. The woman didn't look as if she understood. He kept his voice low, calm, as he took out his cell phone. "I'm going to call 911. The paramedics will take you to the hospital," he promised.

Just then, someone came on the line. Quickly, Laredo rattled off the necessary information to the dispatch operator, giving the woman on the other end Linda Morrow's address and a thumbnail summary of what had transpired.

Flipping the phone closed, he turned toward Taylor. "Didn't expect him to off himself," he was saying, and then his eyes narrowed. She stood with only her profile visible to him, but he didn't like what he saw. "Are you all right?" he asked, crossing to her. "You look a little pale."

"Pale?" she repeated, then pressed her lips together as she could literally *feel* the word echoing inside her brain.

"Yes, pale," he repeated. "As in no color in your face,"

he further elaborated. Linda was calling to him, crying that her leg was burning, but he barely heard the other woman. All his attention was focused on Taylor. His gut tightened as he voiced his worse suspicion. "Taylor, are you hurt?"

"Oh, you might say that," she allowed in a reedy voice, trying her best to sound nonchalant. She knew she was failing. She was just much too weak to carry the charade any further. It felt as if strength was literally draining out of her.

"Where?" Laredo demanded. "Where are you hurt?" Even as he asked, he was lifting up her jacket. Horrified at what he saw, he pulled it from her arms so he could get to her wound more easily.

"Laredo, please, control yourself," she quipped. She tried to smile, but couldn't.

Taylor desperately tried to be flippant, to show Laredo that she was okay. The problem was, she wasn't okay. Not anywhere *near* okay. Her head swirled around like a merry-go-round stuck in fast-forward and nothing was making sense anymore. Her head felt completely out of focus.

"At least wait…wait until we're alone," she joked.

It became a major effort to remain coherent and say each word. Even now, at the end of the sentence, she wasn't sure what she'd just said to him.

Taking a deep breath, she said, "I'm going to go outside to wait for the paramedics." She said it, but she couldn't seem to make her legs obey.

Confused, she looked down at her legs. Why weren't they moving?

The next moment, everything around her went black.

Before Taylor could open her mouth in protest, the blackness found her and swallowed her up.

It was only because of his quick reflexes that Laredo caught her before she hit the floor.

In the background, he heard the distant sound of approaching sirens and silently offered up his first prayer since he was a child.

Chapter 15

"Really, people, you are going to have to clear the hallway!"

The edict was delivered—not for the first time—by Celia Roberts, the no-nonsense, heavyset head nurse who was a twenty-year veteran at Aurora Memorial. She addressed the overwhelming throng that filled the cheerfully decorated surgical waiting room to its maximum capacity and now spilled out into the passageway before the first-floor operating room.

Every adult member of the Cavanaugh family had been there, marking time the entire afternoon. Ever since word had gone out that Taylor had been shot while trying to bring in the "leather strip strangler," as the killer had been dubbed within the department.

Years of practice had the crusty nurse selecting the

most authoritative-looking member of the group and making her appeal to them. In this case, she made a bee-line for Andrew Cavanaugh, who had arrived with his wife shortly after Taylor had been taken into surgery.

"Sir, can't you pick a spokesperson or a go-between who'll keep the rest of you informed?" She scanned the sea of concerned faces. "This is really getting to be a mob scene."

For a moment, Andrew looked sympathetically at the head nurse, but then he surprised her by shaking his head in response to her question.

"I could, but it wouldn't do any good. We're Taylor McIntyre's family and I'm afraid that, orders or no orders, nobody's willing to leave here until we hear something positive."

"Family?" the woman echoed, stunned as her eyes swept over the crowd. "All of you?"

"Every last one," Andrew assured her. "Except for him." He nodded toward Laredo, who stood closest to the O.R.'s swinging doors. "And I sincerely doubt you could get him to leave without resorting to dynamite."

The woman exhaled loudly, her dark brown eye-brows forming a single, disapproving line above the bridge of her nose.

"Having you all out here like this—" she waved her hand around "—is a fire hazard and a violation of the fire code," she insisted.

People far more adept at it had tried to bully him without success. Andrew merely smiled at her and replied, "I know the fire chief. Trust me, you'll get a pass this one time."

Andrew could only pray that it was this one time. That none of his own would ever wind up here like this again: wounded and in need of emergency surgery. But they all knew that getting shot was a very real part of the job description. Even so, it wasn't anything any of them had learned how to live with.

He glanced over toward his brother Brian and Lila, his brother's wife and Taylor's mother. He couldn't remember Lila ever looking quite this pale and drawn, even the time that she herself had been shot and on the verge of death. And her wound had been far more life threatening. But those kinds of facts made no difference to a mother, he thought. Having a child get shot was the basis of nightmares.

"She's going to be fine, Lila," Brian told her. Brian had lost track of how many times he'd said that to his wife since they'd gotten the call from Frank.

Lila hadn't taken her eyes off the operating-room doors since they had gotten here. "I know, I know," she murmured now, grasping her husband's hand and squeezing it for strength. Her own was icy. "It's just that things can always go wrong, even in the best of hospitals." There was a hitch in her voice. "God, I wish they were all insurance claims adjusters—or chefs," she added, glancing over toward Andrew and noting the way her brother-in-law was looking at her, concern etched on his face.

"Then they wouldn't be our kids," Brian pointed out. "Like it or not, Lila, this is the family business—keeping the citizens of Aurora safe."

She exhaled, nodded. "And turning my hair gray while they're at it."

Brian leaned over and pressed a kiss to her temple. "I'd love you even if all your hair fell out and you were bald," he told her. And then, giving her another quick kiss, he nodded over toward the figure at the O.R. doors. "I'm going to go talk to Laredo before he gets it into his head to barge into the O.R."

Lila fell into place beside him. "I'll come with you."

Her voice was hollow. He was worried about her. "Don't get any ideas about the O.R.," Brian warned, only half kidding. Lila wasn't the type to hang back. It was one of the reasons he loved her the way he did.

Lila merely nodded.

Making his way through the crowd over to Laredo it occurred to Brian that the private investigator looked like he was ready to shatter into a hundred brittle pieces. He knew what that felt like. It wasn't all that many years ago that he had been in the exact same position in this hospital, only it was Lila's blood that had been on his clothes. The way Taylor's was now on Laredo's.

"We could try to scrounge up a shirt for you, boy," Brian offered once he was beside Laredo. He nodded at the thirty-four people in the immediate vicinity. "One of us is bound to have a change of clothing in the trunk."

Laredo blinked, turning toward Brian. He realized that the older man was talking to him, but none of the words penetrated. He was lost in a fog. And, for the first time since he was eleven, he was scared that he would lose someone.

Back then, it had been his mother he was terrified of losing. He remembered that he'd hoped against hope, as he rode to the hospital with his grandfather, that the policeman who had called to notify them had gotten it wrong. That the car accident had only been fatal for the other driver, not his mother.

And now, despite the optimistic prognosis that the admitting E.R. doctor had given him, bitter memories of that long-ago day came rushing back at him. He couldn't lose Taylor.

Loving someone was a bitch. But then, he'd already come to that conclusion years ago, at his mother's funeral.

How had this even happened? Laredo silently demanded. He'd been so nonchalant, so laid-back, so convinced that he could handle getting close to this sharp-tongued detective because the doors were left open at both ends. Neither of them wanted a commitment. He knew that for a fact. She'd said so.

So what the hell had happened?

How had he gone from having a good time to having his gut squeezed so hard, it felt as if he was being cut in two by a buzz saw?

Shaking his head now, Laredo looked at Brian. "I'm sorry, what?"

"Your shirt," Brian repeated, pointing to it. "I can scout around to get you something else to wear. Something that's not quite so—vivid," he elaborated. The entire front of Laredo's shirt was covered with Taylor's blood. Made you wonder just how much blood a person could lose and still remain alive, Brian thought uneasily.

Glancing down at his chest as if just now becoming aware that Taylor's blood was smeared over a large part of it, Laredo just shook his head. In some strange way, the bloody shirt made him feel closer to Taylor. "No, thanks, it's okay. It doesn't matter."

Lila gently placed her hand on his arm. "Maybe you should let one of the doctors check you out," she suggested.

Again Laredo shook his head. "No, I'm okay. Really." If anything, his body felt numb all over. And then he saw the torment in Brian's eyes. The burden of guilt he felt was almost more than he could bear.

"I should have never put my gun down," he told the Chief of D's. "I should have just gone ahead and shot the bastard. Damn it, why didn't I?" he upbraided himself angrily.

Brian placed a compassionate hand on Laredo's shoulder. He'd managed to get a very cursory explanation from Laredo when he'd first arrived and one of the first responders on the scene had quickly taken down Laredo's statement, so Brian was aware of the chain of events that had led to finding two dead on the scene and Taylor badly wounded.

"Because you're a decent human being who doesn't just shoot first and ask questions later," Brian told him. "And that is what gives you one up on the bad guys," he pointed out.

"I don't want to be one up on them," Laredo said bitterly, looking at the O.R. doors again. Why wasn't anyone coming out to talk to them? The surgery was taking too long. That couldn't be good. "I just want her to be all right."

"She will be." Brian made the promise so firmly, it

sounded as if his convictions were written in stone. "She will be."

Laredo scrubbed his hands over his face. His brain had turned to mush. "I wish I could believe that."

At that moment, the operating-room doors finally opened and the surgeon walked out. It took less than five seconds for everyone to converge around him.

Dr. Peter Mathias appeared a little surprised at the number of people he saw.

"How is she?" Brian's, Lila's and Laredo's voices mingled together as all three asked the same question at precisely the same time.

"She's a very lucky young woman. The bullet miraculously bypassed all her vital organs. She's going to be fine."

"Can I see her?" Lila asked, her voice throbbing with eagerness.

"Can she have visitors?" Brian asked.

The surgeon addressed the throng of people. "Just one at a time and for only a few minutes. She's still very groggy. Don't be surprised if she falls asleep while you're talking to her." He smiled as he shook his head. "But then, she woke up the second the surgery was over. Tough breed of kids you're raising," he told the petite woman.

"I know." Lila's eyes shone with tears as she took a step forward. And then she stopped to face Laredo. She instinctively knew that this man meant a great deal to her daughter. Apparently more than most. And, judging by the look on Laredo's face, the feeling was mutual. "Would you like to go in first?" she offered.

"No, it's okay," Laredo assured her. "I just wanted to

make sure Taylor was going to pull through. Tell her—
tell her—" He realized that he had no idea what message
he wanted to pass on. Joyful and miserable at the same
time, he'd never felt so damn confused in his life. Seeing
Taylor unconscious and bleeding had turned everything
inside out. "Tell her I'm glad she's okay."

Laredo was about to weave his way through the
crowd in order to leave, but Brian caught him by the
arm. Laredo eyed the chief of detectives.

"Why don't you tell her yourself?" Brian suggested.
And then, lowering his voice, he added, "There are
some things you just can't run from, boy. And you'd be
better off if you don't even try. Trust me."

There was no point in arguing. Laredo knew Brian
was right. Taking a breath, he nodded. "Thanks."

Going through the maze of corridors, which were as
confusing as his thoughts, Laredo followed a talkative
orderly to the room that Taylor had been taken to after
the operation.

When he entered the single care unit, Laredo saw that
Taylor's eyes were shut.

"You asleep?" he asked. There was no response. "Guess
so." He began to back out, then stopped. There were things
he needed to say, to purge out of his system, and what
better time to do it than when she couldn't really hear him?

"Damn it, Taylor, you gave me one hell of a scare
back there." And then he laughed shortly. "For more
reasons than one, I guess." He dragged an impatient
hand through his hair. "I thought you were going to die.
And if you did, everything would just stop. The sun, the

world, everything would just go away. At least for me."
He looked at all the IV tubes attached to her, all the
monitors documenting every step of her progress. "This
wasn't supposed to happen. You weren't supposed to get
shot and more than that, I wasn't supposed to feel this
way about you," he insisted. "Like I couldn't breathe in
a world that you weren't in. I'm not supposed to feel
things. I *promised* myself I wasn't going to feel things."
He glanced out the window. The sky had darkened in
anticipation of night. "There's no room in my world for
feelings. All they do is mess everything up and get in
the way. I can't deal with that."

He looked back down at her. Her eyes were still
closed so he continued. "I can't deal with worrying,
wondering if this is the last time I am going to see you.
That's not me, you hear me? That's not me."

Biting off a curse, he turned to go.

He hadn't realized just how closely he'd been standing
next to her bed. When he turned to walk out, he found
that the bottom of his shirt was caught on something.

Expecting to see something sticking out from her
hospital bed, a jagged edge on the side rails or something like that, Laredo was surprised to discover that the
reason he couldn't leave was because Taylor's fingers
were wrapped around a section of his shirt.

"Taylor?" he questioned in surprise.

It was then, as he bent even closer to peer at her, that
he saw her eyes flutter open. Her lips moved, but he
couldn't hear what she said.

"What?" he asked urgently, bending even closer. His
ear was almost next to her lips.

That was when he heard them. The two words she uttered hoarsely.

"Me, too."

Stunned, he straightened. "Taylor?"

Her fingers became lax, slipping from his shirt, telling him that she had slipped back into unconsciousness.

He stood watching her for a few moments. And then he left.

He didn't come back.

Not during her hospital stay nor during her convalescence, spent, at their insistence, entirely at her parents' house.

In the two weeks since she had been shot, Taylor hadn't heard even a single word from Laredo. At times, his non-appearance made her sincerely doubt that she had heard what she thought she'd heard that day after her surgery. Those times she chalked up her "memory" to the aftermath of the anesthesia, or maybe to hallucinations.

At other times, she was certain she *had* heard him.

And, in an odd way, the fact that he hadn't come to see her proved it.

When she was finally strong enough to move back into her own apartment, her parents, two brothers and sister all came with her. She patiently waited for them all to leave, turning down their offers, tendered one at a time, to spend the first night back with her. The moment they were gone, she sneaked back out to her carport and got in behind the wheel of her car.

She'd missed her independence. And she was about to do something to surrender it again, she thought. Willingly.

Starting up her car, Taylor drove over to Laredo's apartment.

He wasn't home.

Frustrated, she thought about coming back later, then decided to have this out with him once and for all. Making sure no one was around to observe her, she quickly let herself into his apartment, utilizing the skills she'd picked up from her dealings with the less-than-straight-and-narrow people she'd encountered on the street.

It was past seven o'clock and Laredo was bone-tired when he finally got home. But, bone-weary or not, he was instantly alert the second he put his hand on the doorknob. It gave. He *always* locked the door when he left.

Drawing his weapon, Laredo entered the apartment cautiously, prepared to go from room to room, searching for the intruder.

He didn't have far to look. Whoever had come in was still there, sitting on a recliner in the living room. He could just make out the outline of someone in the shadows. Adrenaline roaring through his veins, Laredo flipped the switch, bathing the room in light. He blinked.

Taylor?

No, it couldn't be. His imagination had just kicked into overdrive, that's all.

Terrific.

"Damn it," he muttered angrily, holstering his weapon, "now I'm seeing her."

His comment and the sudden influx of light roused Taylor, who'd dozed off waiting for him. The moment she opened her eyes, they blazed.

"So, you're not dead," she declared as if the discovery was news to her. "I guess that means you're a coward."

Ambivalent feelings battled it out inside her as she rose to her feet. Part of her wanted to throw her arms around him and the other part wanted to throw her hands around his throat for an entirely different reason.

"I figured those were the only two viable options why you didn't come back to see me. You were either dead or a coward. I figured the first was a definite possibility. But I never thought that you might actually be a coward." Disappointment entered her eyes. "I guess I was wrong."

Despite the fact that he'd applied the term to himself several times, he took offense when she did it. "I'm not a coward."

Doubling her fists and digging them into her hips, Taylor glared at him. "Then why didn't you come back to see me?"

He did his best to seem distant. It wasn't easy when all he wanted to do, despite her insults, was to hold her. To bury his face in her hair and inhale the fragrance he knew was there. "The case was over."

Taylor stared at him. She felt her heart splintering. Let that be a lesson to her. Falling in love was tantamount to a death wish. "And that's it?" she heard herself say.

Damn it, woman, why didn't you stay away? "What else is there?"

"Oh, I don't know." Rising on her toes, she was in his face. Some instinct that went deeper than her fear of being hurt said, "Love, maybe."

"Love?" He said the word as if he'd never heard it before. As if, even now, it wasn't eating up his very insides.

"Yeah, love," she repeated. She curbed her desire to beat on him with her fists. Why was he doing this to her? To them? "You said you loved me."

He shook his head, moving away. He became overly interested in removing his weapon and holster. "You were hallucinating."

Taylor moved until she was in front of him again. She wasn't about to allow him to avoid her. "No, I wasn't. And the fact of the matter is, I love you, too, you big dumb jerk, and I want to know what you're going to do about it."

"Do about it?" he echoed. Suddenly, he felt a smile struggling to take over his mouth. Taylor loved him? "What do you want me to do about it?" he asked her.

Taylor shook her head. The ball was in his court and the next move was his. Some things even an independent woman needed a man to do.

"Oh, no, you first."

He took her hand in his, drawing her closer to him. Enfolding her in his arms. Every fiber in his body came alive. Oh, God, but he had missed this. Missed her. The clouds began to lift, disappearing as if they'd never existed. "You love me, too, huh?"

She rolled her eyes. "That's what I said. At least you have decent hearing."

He smiled down into her face. This wasn't nearly as hard as he thought it was going to be. A lot less difficult than imagining his life without her. "How do you feel about marriage?"

Taylor felt her heart skip a beat, but she refused to get ahead of herself. Refused to put words into his mouth. "In general or specifically?"

He laughed, shaking his head. "Damn, for a cop, you sound like a lawyer. Specifically," Laredo underscored, then added, "ours," when she didn't say anything.

She looked at him, puzzled. Had she missed something, or was this some side effect from the medications she'd been taking after her surgery? "We don't have a marriage."

He skimmed his lips along her forehead. "Yet."

She felt herself growing warm. "Are you asking me to marry you?"

And now he grinned at her. "That would seem to be the direction this is going in, yes."

Just because she wasn't shy and retiring didn't mean she didn't want all the trappings that went with something like this. "Damn it, Laredo, say something romantic."

"Something romantic," he echoed, then ducked as she swung to hit him. Catching her in his arms again, he held her close. "Marry me, Taylor. Marry me and make my life a little less miserable than it is right now."

She sighed. So much for a honeyed tongue. "You *can't* say something romantic, can you?"

He lifted his shoulder in a half shrug. "I figure, if you say yes, I've got the next forty years to practice."

"Only forty?"

"After that, we'll negotiate." Warm rays of sunshine threaded all through him. He hadn't thought that it was possible to feel this happy. It almost seemed as if it should be against the law. "Don't want you to get too complacent."

She had a feeling that was never going to happen. Not if she was married to him.

"So?" he coaxed. "Are you going to say yes?"

She laced her arms around his neck, thinking how much she'd missed being this close to him. "Don't rush me, I'm thinking about it."

He kissed her softly even as he began to undress her. "Think fast."

She managed to say yes before they both became too busy to talk.

Epilogue

Reuniting with Taylor, Laredo handed her one of the two glasses of eggnog he'd gone to fetch. Because the noise level in the living room was swelling to epic proportions, he leaned down so that his lips were closer to her ear. "Finished making the rounds?" he asked her.

She laughed, taking a sip. "Not even close."

This was Andrew's annual Christmas party. Not only had the entire extended family shown up, but it felt like at least half the force was here as well. There were people in almost every room, not to mention that they were spilling out into the backyard.

Suddenly jostled from behind, Taylor clutched her drink with both hands to keep it from spilling.

"Sorry," Zach apologized, flashing his sister a grin before merging into the crowd.

"You know, there'd be more room here if the chief had invited less people or gotten a smaller tree," Laredo observed.

Finishing his eggnog, he put the glass down on the closest flat surface and looked up at the heavily decorated tree. It stood more than ten feet tall, thanks to the cathedral ceilings, and there was a story behind each and every one of the countless decorations that hung on every available branch.

Laredo shook his head. "That has got to be the biggest Christmas tree I've ever seen outside of a mall."

Finishing her own drink, Taylor placed her empty glass next to his. "This coming from a man who doesn't even put a tree up."

He shrugged carelessly, drawing her over to a doorway and away from, for the time being, the immediate flow of foot traffic. "It's still early."

She pinned him with a look. "It's Christmas Eve."

"That's my point," he said innocently. "There's still tomorrow."

Yeah, right. "You're planning on putting a tree up tonight?"

He pretended to think it over. "Well, doesn't seem like it's worth the trouble for just one day, does it?"

"It's *always* worth the trouble." Taylor shook her head. She absolutely loved Christmas and the celebration of the holiday was deeply entrenched in her soul. "You should have a tree."

He took hold of her hands in his. "Why?"

Taylor sighed. "If I have to explain it, it loses something." Even so, she tried to get him to come around.

"Don't you just light up inside whenever you look, *really* look, at a Christmas tree?"

This time, he was the one who was jostled. He took the opportunity to move in closer to her. "I don't need a tree to light up," Laredo told her, looking down into her eyes. "I have you."

Taylor could feel herself melting. "That has got to be the nicest thing you've ever said to me."

He grinned in response. "Wait," he told her, pointing up directly over her head. There was mistletoe hanging in the doorway. "There's more."

And then, to underscore his promise and because tradition demanded it, Laredo kiss her. Long and hard.

* * * * *

*Bestselling author Lynne Graham is back
with a fabulous new trilogy!*

PREGNANT BRIDES

Three ordinary girls—naïve, but also honest and plucky...

*Three fabulously wealthy, impossibly handsome
and very ruthless men...*

*When opposites attract and passion leads to pregnancy...
it can only mean marriage!*

*Available next month from Harlequin Presents®:
the first installment*

DESERT PRINCE, BRIDE OF INNOCENCE

* * *

'THIS EVENING I'm flying to New York for two weeks,'
Jasim imparted with a casualness that made her heart sink
like a stone. 'That's why I had you brought here. I own this
apartment and you'll be comfortable here while I'm abroad.'

'I can afford my own accommodation although I may not
need it for long. I'll have another job by the time you
get back—'

Jasim released a slightly harsh laugh. 'There's no need for
you to look for another position. How would I ever see you?
Don't you understand what I'm offering you?'

Elinor stood very still. 'No, I must be incredibly thick
because I haven't quite worked out yet what you're offering
me....'

His charismatic smile slashed his lean dark visage.
'Naturally, I want to take care of you....'

HPEX0110A

'No, thanks.' Elinor forced a smile and mentally willed him not to demean her with some sordid proposition. 'The only man who will ever take *care* of me with my agreement will be my husband. I'm willing to wait for you to come back but I'm not willing to be kept by you. I'm a very independent woman and what I give, I give freely.'

Jasim frowned. 'You make it all sound so serious.'

'What happened between us last night left pure chaos in its wake. Right now, I don't know whether I'm on my head or my heels. I'll stay for a while because I have nowhere else to go in the short term. So maybe it's good that you'll be away for a while.'

Jasim pulled out his wallet to extract a card. 'My private number,' he told her, presenting her with it as though it was a precious gift, which indeed it was. Many women would have done just about anything to gain access to that direct hotline to him, but his staff guarded his privacy with scrupulous care.

Before he could close the wallet, his blood ran cold in his veins. How could he have made such a serious oversight? What if he had got her pregnant? He knew that an unplanned pregnancy would engulf his life like an avalanche, crush his freedom and suffocate him. He barely stilled a shudder at the threat of such an outcome and thought how ironic it was that what his older brother had longed and prayed for to secure the line to the throne should strike Jasim as an absolute disaster....

* * *

What will proud Prince Jasim do if Elinor is expecting his royal baby? Perhaps an arranged marriage is the only solution! But will Elinor agree? Find out in DESERT PRINCE, BRIDE OF INNOCENCE by Lynne Graham [#2884], available from Harlequin Presents® in January 2010.

Bestselling Harlequin Presents author

Lynne Graham

brings you an exciting new miniseries:

PREGNANT BRIDES

Inexperienced and expecting, they're forced to marry

Collect them all:

DESERT PRINCE, BRIDE OF INNOCENCE

January 2010

RUTHLESS MAGNATE, CONVENIENT WIFE

February 2010

GREEK TYCOON, INEXPERIENCED MISTRESS

March 2010

Welcome to Montana—the home of bold men and
daring women, where tales of passion, adventure
and intrigue unfold beneath the Big Sky.

Rogue Stallion by DIANA PALMER

Undaunted by rogue cop Sterling McCallum's heart of
stone and his warnings to back off, Jessica Larson stands
her ground, braving the rising emotions between them
until the mystery of his past comes to the surface.

Montana ★ MAVERICKS™

RETURN TO BIG SKY COUNTRY

Available in January 2010 wherever you buy books.

COMING NEXT MONTH

Available December 29, 2009

#1591 CRIMINAL DECEPTION—Marilyn Pappano
The last person Joe Saldana expects to see again is Liz Dalton—his twin brother's ex-girlfriend. They'd once shared an almost-moment, and the spark is clearly still alive. But is his brother? Liz—and a slew of other people—are looking for him, and Joe swears he knows nothing. Is he hiding information? And when he finds out the truth about Liz, will their reignited spark fizzle in the face of danger, secrets and lies?

#1592 THE AGENT'S PROPOSITION—Lyn Stone
Special Ops
By-the-book agent Tess Bradshaw must convince Cameron Cochran to help her bring down a hacker threatening to shut off power across the eastern seaboard. When Cameron decides to use her as bait, they change her image, and the sexy makeover helps her release her inhibitions—in Cameron's bed. Mercenaries and a hurricane threaten their newfound passion, forcing them to choose between love and duty.

#1593 THE PRIVATE BODYGUARD—Debra Cowan
The Hot Zone
He'd died shortly after their relationship had ended, so Dr. Meredith Boren is shocked to discover her ex-fiancé at her lake house, bleeding from a gunshot wound. Gage Parrish has been in Witness Protection, but someone knows he's still alive. Now Meredith is in danger, and he vows to keep her safe. Desperate for a second chance, can he win her back before someone kills them both?

#1594 A DOCTOR'S WATCH—Vickie Taylor
She's not crazy. That's what single mom Mia Serrat keeps trying to tell everyone, but when she's hospitalized after an "accidental" fall, Dr. Ty Hansen is the only one who believes her. Ty avoids becoming involved with patients, but there's something about Mia that's different, and he can't help his protective instincts when her life is jeopardized. He's her only chance at survival, and he'll stop at nothing to save her.